Bangkok Delusions

Zach J Brodsky

BRODSKY PRESS

www.zachjbrodsky.com

ISBN 978-1-9164938-1-0

DEDICATION AND ACKNOWLEDGEMENTS

This book is dedicated to my parents who have always been so supportive and given me all the opportunities in life. Apologies for some of the more vulgar and crude passages of this effort!.

Many thanks to Robert for his advice, critical appraisals on reading sections and his constant imploring me to finish this. I hope it will amuse.

Finally, huge thanks to my editor, Luciano, who painstakingly analysed commas and semi-colons and the like. They say no-one knows semi-colons like Luciano knows semi-colons, and they're not wrong!

Glossary of Thai Words

Bpaak waan – literally sweet mouth, used to describe insincere sweet talkers
Chok dee – good luck
Farang – foreigner
Isaan – Thailand's most populous region in the North East
Khaw jai - understand
Khun – A polite prefix to a name, Mr/Miss etc.
Kidteung – when you miss someone
Mak – very when added to an adjective
Mamasan – the woman who runs a bar with women for hire.
Nong – A prefix before the name of someone younger
Pee – A prefix before the name of someone older
Sawat dii – Hello/ Good Morning
Somtam – A traditional spicy Thai salad made from green papaya
Soi – road
Ting tong - crazy
Yaba – Literally 'crazy drug' a cheap local amphetamine derivative
Ya ice – local name for crystal methamphetamine

ONE

The bright lights dazzled Scotty Marshall as he weaved his way through the throngs of street hawkers. Everything imaginable seemed to be for sale on the streets of Bangkok; deep fried insects, wild animals, noodles and all sorts of other paraphernalia. That's what the guidebooks had informed him in advance, and while it was partially true, the reality was a little less exotic. Most of the people getting in the way of the hefty American seemed to be selling t-shirts, fake Viagra, and other assorted tat. Marshall had only been wandering for 20 minutes but it was already appearing slightly less quirky and fascinating. He wanted to settle down with a nice cool beer and think about his plans for 2 weeks of pure relaxation in Thailand.

He stumbled on the kerb as a noodle seller pushed his heavy cart home. He'd hit that time when the day-time stalls were packing up, but almost automatically night time food places were unloading their bits and pieces, in advance of a long night cooking food for the drunk and desperate who spend their baht in Nana's bars.

An elderly local shouted something and gesticulated at Scotty, who looked back with a questioning tone before he realised the guy was trying to unload bags of uncooked noodles onto the stretch of road that was about to become a temporary restaurant. Scotty gave an apologetic smile, which came out as more of a grimace and headed down the road he had been recommended by a friend who had visited a couple of years earlier.

Nana was the most infamous area of Bangkok sleaze, scrap that, it was *one* of the most infamous areas of Bangkok sleaze. The road was lined with bars and gaudy bright neon lights, while girls perched on chairs outside trying to entice the punters in. There were specialist bars for every taste, although the real specialist places were only discovered after months or even years exploring. Marshall glanced at the flashing lights of 'Princesses' - a ladyboy bar where some of the most beautiful of Nana's girls catered for those 'straight' guys who just liked their beautiful women to have, shall we say, a hint of masculinity. Although of course many of the girls here had got rid of the last memories of their male past many years ago. He had no idea the leggy hostesses were born male, but he didn't like the look of the place anyway, a bit too dark and squalid inside, so he continued to stutter and dodge his way deeper into the Nana abyss.

For newcomers and old-Bangkok hands alike there is something extraordinary about Nana, there can be few places in the urban world that are more difficult to get your head around. It spins and buzzes, there's humour, fun, escapism, and right next to it there is appalling sleaze and exploitation. You have vile sleaze ball scumbags drinking with 'normal' guys on a good night out. There are tourists there just to see what goes on, and there are many simply there for people watching, amateur anthropologists if you will, fascinated to see every facet of human life, here, on and around this one street.

For the people watcher, the side alleys are the crème de la crème. It is here where you can patiently see the heart of what makes Nana tick; sex. Perch against a quiet outdoor bar within eye shot of a couple of 'short-time' hotels, the sort that many customers don't even need the full hour they pay for, and you can learn it all.

Scotty Marshall had only been in Bangkok a couple of days and he was still blissfully naïve about some of what was going on, he didn't really observe the steady stream of couples who walked past him. On his previous night down this road he didn't even notice the same ladyboy enter the 'Nana House Hotel' 3 times in the space of 90 minutes with different customers.

The punters here displayed a fascinating array of behaviour types. You had the 'distance' ones – they always kept 3-5 feet in front or behind the girls they had just purchased before doing a quick rush into the chosen hotel, trying to hide their shame at what they were doing. You had the ludicrously over-friendly ones, laughing and joking with their new girl so that perhaps one could think they were old friends, or a couple in love and in a long-term relationship. Then you had the ones who had probably been through those phases, and were now old enough and grey enough to think 'fuck it, we all know what's going on here.' They'd walk in arm-in-arm, hand on ass, perfectly at ease with the fact that they had just bought an hour's worth of fun. Marshall noticed none of it, he was still in awe of the whole scene, he was still battling the sweat patches that were spreading further and further down his back and armpits and he was still wondering just what the fuck he was doing with his life.

There is an intensity to Nana that Scott Marshall was slowly starting to realise. The oppressive heat merely added to the sense of drama and feel that the place was on edge, on the verge of something significant. Somewhere on this *soi* there was always a story developing. A blossoming 'love' story, and perhaps in the same bar a wilting romance. Some wilted to such an extent that there were unpleasant or violent repercussions.

Many classifications consider Bangkok as the hottest city in the world. There may be other places where the mercury rises higher, but in those places the temperature can plummet at times too. Not so in Bangkok. With the bright lights and fierce air conditioning units running 24/7 it's rare for the temperature to dip much below 30 degrees centigrade, ever. On its hottest nights you can feel the heaviness in the atmosphere. Fans blow the hot air around and in Nana poorly functioning A/C units add to the humidity. To top it all you have scantily clad women holding everything together yet teetering on the brink with testosterone charged men prowling at every vantage point. Marshall battled on intrigued, thirsty and becoming enticed by the heavily sexualised atmosphere

Scotty Marshall, like so many who find respite in the dark reaches of Bangkok's underbelly was at something of a low ebb, to put it mildly his life was a mess.

Marshall was born while his dad (Scott Marshall!) was out fighting in Vietnam. Even for many Americans that was an utterly futile war, a tragedy and terrible precursor for what the world was to become. The Marshalls didn't see it that way. A fiercely patriotic family with a history immersed in the military they saw it as their great nation doing their thing. Scott Marshall Senior had never been prouder than the day his son signed up for the US Army, apart from perhaps the day 'junior' went to Iraq and experienced real combat.

Scotty Marshall returned from that first Gulf War with a real swagger, confident to the point of arrogant. He had a triumphant air; the US was still running the world and sticking it to foreigners. It was in that air that he met Brenda and swept her off her feet. They were married a year later. Sadly for Brenda the fit, confident man she had fallen for, had all but gone within a few years of marriage.

They slipped into a comfortable domestic life, had some kids, bought a house in a nice residential suburb. To outsiders they *were* the American dream. Brenda however, was full of regret. She looked back and felt her life was a missed opportunity. She never pursued the career she wanted. She married the first man she had vaguely liked. She did what society expected of her. It was only after joining a book club and meeting a new circle of friends that she felt empowered enough to take control of her life.

For most of their marriage she had felt fairly indifferent to Scotty, but towards the end she was starting to positively dislike him. She had moved on in life. He hadn't. When she finally told him that she wanted a divorce he was shocked and stunned. That summed him up for Brenda. How can he not have known? Their conversations were all small talk. They had no physical relationship to speak of anymore. Their kids had grown up. Why would they stay together?

The break up hit Marshall hard. When he left the army Brenda replaced the sergeants in running his life. He felt helpless. He realised that his social life was totally managed by her. Suddenly he was living alone in a small apartment desperately trying to reconnect with old buddies. It was one of those buddies who told him that a couple of weeks in Bangkok would totally rejuvenate him.

It was on this night, only his 3rd in Bangkok that Marshall's life would change forever. Not just with the benefit of hindsight. When he woke up the next morning he began to write a diary. He hadn't done that since high school, but he'd read on various self-help websites that writing down your inner thoughts was a great first step to sorting your life out.

Dear Diary, (Do I really write this?)

Tonight I met my dream girl. I wandered down that road I'd been told about, and it was then that I saw her. A shy innocence in her dark eyes. She didn't belong there, that was evident. She was something magical, special among this madness. I went over to her and introduced myself with the

Thai that I had learnt "Sawat dii, my name Scotty, me American." She smiled and I knew instantly she could see I was also someone who didn't belong on this dingy street. She smiled the sweetest smile and said the words that made the hairs on the back of my neck stand up. "My name Ting."

The heat was stifling and the noise and bright lights would have made me feel dizzy anyway, but Ting was enough to make any red-blooded American man weak at the knees. It was immediately clear that what Ting and I lacked in shared language skills we made up for in the unspoken language of love. I was in love and Ting knew it, she was smitten with me. "I buy you drink?" I nervously asked. What if she refused? This was the girl of my dreams. A woman I was already imagining spending the rest of my life with. I knew the next few seconds could change my life. I could feel a bead of sweat wind its way down my neck and into the small of my back, another started to drip down my forehead. Time stopped. Ting looked at me. Did I detect a smile from her sweet lips? "Yes, I like." I had to compose myself not to burst into tears right then and there. Finally a woman who saw me for what I was. A beautiful kind man and not just a 50-something, overweight, divorced ex-US Army combatant with 2 kids who hated him and an ex-wife embracing her new life and being happier than ever, without me.

I didn't need to ask Ting her drink of choice, the connection was so strong. I ordered her a Leo Ice Shake, yes folks in Bangkok you could get a beer slushy. I held my cool Heineken to my temple to cool me down. Ting giggled and made me melt, "you good man, handsome." Right then I would have done anything for Ting and she knew it. Ting nervously sipped her drink, I can tell she knows this is the start of something special. I smiled at her, she smiled back. Although this was our first date we were already comfortable with the silence. I had never experienced anything like this, and I'd experienced plenty of women in my time in the US Army, that's for sure. Yet here I am, 54 year old Scotty 'one-shot' Marshall writing a teenage diary and reduced to a sweating wreck by a young Thai goddess. I asked Ting how long she had visited bars in Nana. "Not long time much", there was something so endearing about the way she used English. We chatted deep into the evening, Ting told me how most of the girls in this bar were working as hookers. She then explained that she had never gone home with someone she met in a bar, she just couldn't do that, it would be disrespectful to her family who were struggling to make ends meet in their small village in Thailand's rural Northeast. We'd only spent an hour together but I could already see a change in Ting, her life was changing before my very eyes. "Maybe I want go home with you."

I had to pinch myself. I was living a Hollywood love story. Here I am, my first few days in Bangkok and the most beautiful, shy and innocent woman was telling me that she was feeling things she too had never felt. I waved my 100-baht note and called over the slightly stern faced woman who ran the bar. I ordered another Heineken. "You buy drink for Ting." Ting looked embarrassed "I never drink two drink before." I gave the lady a 20-baht tip, enough money to buy herself a meal, no doubt. I could see my polite manner was starting to impress Ting even further.

After another hour of gazing into each other's eyes, I told Ting I had to go back to my hotel to sleep. Ting suddenly looked forlorn and upset "you not like me Khun Scott?" I tried to explain to Ting that I would come and see her again on another night. A tear formed in her eye, and she told me that she did not have enough money to pay her rent, and hoped to come and stay in my hotel. Her landlord would be after the 500 baht she owed. I felt guilty but offered Ting the money, I knew a girl like Ting would never accept charity from a stranger. She refused, but I managed to persuade her that I *wanted to help. "Friends help each other Ting, and I think we will be very close friends."*

"You nice fat man.". I started to walk back to my hotel in a daze, with a big grin on my face, oblivious to the hordes of working girls trying to entice me into their bars. There is no-one like Ting.

TWO

As Scotty snaked his way through the streets he suddenly realised he was in an unfamiliar location. He had tried to carefully remember the fifteen minute walk from the hotel but with the bright lights and thoughts of Ting uppermost in his mind, he started to amble in a daydream trying to re-track his short walk. Suddenly he was standing in a small alleyway with a few seedy hotels and an outdoor bar.

He must have looked quite a sight. Sweating profusely, he lacked any genuine sartorial eloquence. Smart black dress shoes with white socks pulled too far up his shins. His baggy, beige khaki shorts were certainly informal but he wore a relatively smart white shirt (translucent in places from the sweat), tightly tucked in. To cap it all he had his mobile phone strapped to his belt in that gun-holster style that was unfathomable to most people. He stood and pondered.

A tall British guy staggered out of one of the hotels and slapped a ladyboy on her backside as he handed her a crumpled 1,000 baht note. He barked at her in slurred, barely audible tones

"15 fabulous minutes, you're an angel." Just then a shorter drunk guy slumped on the table looked up and shouted.

"Oi, Bobby Lowe… is that you? You old dog!" The ladyboy's customer cleaned his glasses and tried to focus.

"Alf Hayes, as I live and breathe, how the hell are you?" Lowe grimaced and tried to clear something from deep in his throat.

"Good lord man I wouldn't expect to find you around here, I've not seen you here since, well good lord, let me think….."

"Yeh yeh, I've had a couple of nights off…" Hayes smiled with an infectious grin right across his face and welcomed his scruffier friend to join him at the table.

They continued this mock catch up conversation, it eventually became clear to Scotty that they were friends who obviously spent most of their time in these bars. He stood there fixed to the ground, lost in the Bangkok underworld.

The shorter man looked up at, and spoke in a thick London accent "Do we have a newbie lost in the Big Mango? Pull up a chair squire and share some old war stories with me and my good mate Bobby Lowe".

It was 1am, Scotty was tired but he thought these guys might be able to help him find his way out of this alcohol fuelled metropolis. He explained his predicament. Lowe looked totally puzzled, bewildered almost as he pulled a handful of crumpled notes out of his pocket, and tried to work out how many more beers he could buy.

Hayes chuckled. "Aha classic newbie mistake, you've gone all the way to the top of *Soi* 4 by mistake. You should have cut through the Diamond Bar, come out into the sideway at the top of *soi* 6, cut down the alley and sneaked through the fried rice stall. Would have taken you right up to the door of your hotel, "Honeypuss House Hotel".

Hayes had a grin on his face and added "wise choice of hotel too, some lovely skirt working in the downstairs bar there." He leaned back and his grin took on a more sinister nuance as the Londoner appeared to be remembering some of his experiences with the 'skirt' at the Honeypuss House Hotel.

Meanwhile Bob Lowe was lost in his pathetic counting game, notes were flung about and every time the decrepit fan worked its way back to point towards the table he frantically had to trap the notes and start counting again.

"What's a beer here again Alf?" grumbled Lowe. "Here?" replied Hayes, "well it's much the same as elsewhere my old mate, fermented hops and other bits and bobs." The joke was lost on Lowe, who just gave a look of utter confusion.

Hayes looked at Lowe as one might look at an injured dog on the road, dipped his hand in his pocket and handed Lowe 500 baht. Lowe hugged him and assured him this was the last loan he needed. Hayes grinned.

Alf Hayes had been living in Bangkok for getting on 15 years, and he ran a quiet but profitable money lending business. He was always to be found within a mile or so radius of the Nana area. He was an easy man to find, you only had to pop into a few bars and ask if 'Big' Alf was about and a young bar girl would point you in the right direction, or at least point you towards someone who would know. The money-lending side of operations was the closest Alf Hayes could get to a 'respectable' business front. Over the years in Bangkok he had brokered himself into a relatively strong position in the illegal drug trade in the Nana area, albeit by luck more than judgement or skills. He controlled much of Sukhumvit *Soi* 4 and its off-shoots having reached an amicable agreement with two Thais who also had a stronghold in the area. Hayes had actually shown some impressive, almost political manoeuvrings after the shooting of thousands of Bangkok's dealers in the infamous crackdown on drugs during a previous government administration. Within weeks Hayes had gone from petty dealer to pseudo drug baron, in his own mind at least. The reality was that Hayes was making a decent living from drugs, but he had a burning desire to be Thailand's answer to Pablo Escobar, and didn't quite know how to achieve that. He had read about the volumes of cash that Escobar had been dealing with in his prime, and dreamed of being in such an esteemed position.

Hayes looked every bit his 53 years and more, with a weathered look, the sort that Bangkok seemed to specialise in among its foreign guests. Hayes' hair was seriously thinning and while he wasn't quite doing a combover it looked like he didnt have any idea how to deal with the inevitable hairline recession of a man of his age. His story was not a dissimilar one to many who called this part of Bangkok 'home'. He came to Bangkok for a holiday with mates and found himself hooked. Cheap beer, cheap girls. For a single man in his mid-30s who felt his appeal to British girls was diminishing by the day he suddenly felt desirable. A year later when he was offered voluntary redundancy from the mundane IT role he had at a major British company, he booked himself a flight to Bangkok with a plan to see what happened. He took himself a couple of gigs teaching English in the early days. Language schools, Thai schools, whatever he found. By night he drunk in Nana or *Soi* Cowboy, virtually every night. Six or seven nights a week was his norm.

The money lending happened by chance. He lent a fellow *farang* 10,000 baht one night. The poor chap had been stopped by the police outside the bar Hayes was boozing in, with an illegal substance in his possession. He didn't have enough money on him or in his bank to bribe the police. His choice was simple. Hand the police 20,000 baht there and then or go down the police station and be charged. He was 10k short of what he needed and so Alf Hayes obliged. The guy was a Nana acquaintance and Hayes felt it was the right thing to do. Two weeks later the chap re-paid Hayes giving him 12,000 and buying him a few beers, such was his gratitude. Two thousand baht extra to avoid a long time in prison was pretty cheap. With that 'Alf Hayes – money lender', was born.

Yes, Alf Hayes became relatively well known in this small area of town. In *his* mind he had become a Bangkok legend. His customers (for both drugs and money) ranged from middle class Thai business types to foreigners working in town and noodle stall cooks. To some onlookers he had a heart of gold - the girls who plied their trade in Bangkok's bars always knew Hayes would give them a low-interest or even at times an interest free loan. In many cases he would tell them not to worry about paying it all back, not in cash anyway, but Alf Hayes always got paid back. He made sure of that.

Hayes leaned back in his chair and gave his ample gut a loving pat, and looked at his friend Bob 'the cat' Lowe. Over the years Alf Hayes had lent literally thousands and thousands of baht to the hopeless Bob Lowe. Lowe was a lovable, affable chap, but a classic Bangkok story. He came to Bangkok fresh faced to teach English, like so many do. Within 5 years he was economically trapped in Thailand, never able to earn enough for a flight home and addicted to the sex and booze that was readily available on the streets of the Big Mango. For a number of years Hayes insisted on full control of Lowe's bank accounts in a desperate attempt to bring some sanity to Bob's life. It didn't work, Hayes tired of the pitiful, tearful 3am phone calls and another pregnant bar girl who needed money for an abortion. Somehow Lowe managed to keep his head above water. Gone were the days of comfortable condominiums, Lowe lived in something akin to a squat, but at just a few thousand baht a month you didn't hear him complaining.
"This way them girls know I've not got a pot to piss in, and they'll never bother me for more than one night." There wasn't a bar girl in Bangkok who didn't know of Bob Lowe, and his remarkable ability to down pints. As the legend had it Lowe once went out on Christmas Eve and returned home in early January, if it were anyone but Bob Lowe you'd think this was an urban legend, but that was Lowe.

Marshall enjoyed chatting with Alf and Bob, and

shared with them his evening, which he considered amazing. He sensed a glance between the two British men, and on more than one occasion Bob Lowe bellowed "be careful man, we've all been there." The quieter Hayes just nodded in agreement.

The following day when writing in his diary, Marshall added:

It was then that I realised that Hayes and Lowe hadn't been there, they can't possibly have experienced what I did tonight. If they had they couldn't have been so cynical. I told them that Ting was not a bar girl, but merely a girl visiting a bar for a drink. I definitely saw Hayes' eyebrows rise. What did he know? I know what he didn't know, he didn't know Ting.

After they settled their bill, Hayes offered to take Scotty back to his hotel. "Been a while since I've been down to the Honeypuss. They may have some new girls in." Hayes shimmied around the *sois* with a nimble footed assuredness that could only have come from years of exploration. Scotty had no idea he was so near to his hotel. The Honeypuss House was a sweet sight for his drunken New Jersey eyes, and he stumbled up to his room, falling asleep almost instantly, with dreams of the sweet Ting.

It was now close to 3am, a time when Nana begins to edge towards calming down. If the heat drops at all it's now that you might start to feel it. Alf Hayes sat down for a final beer at Honeypuss and decided if there was anything decent he'd buy himself a quickie, a bit of light relief before trudging back home to sleep.

A heavily pregnant woman was trying a hard-sell

with two arrogant twenty-something Brits. Hayes heard one of them utter "look at the state of you, talk about low grade hookers." His buddy high-fived him and laughed as they continued to toy with the woman. Hayes walked over.

"Something funny boys? Finish your beers and fuck off before I call big Boom over there to deal with the pair of you." He indicated towards an intimidating muscular man inside the bar. He looked at the girl.

"Now you. Have some fucking self-respect. Think about your bastard kid."

He gave her 1000 baht and gestured her to go home. He was pretty certain he'd had a night with her a couple of years earlier, but he couldn't be sure.

THREE

It was just after 3am when Ting packed her few things into her handbag; a make-up kit, and various random bits and pieces. Another shit night in her shit life she thought to herself. She hadn't made enough and had wasted hours with that fat American guy for only 500 baht. 'Play the long game' the words of her mentor, Pinky, went around in her head. She was impressed with herself, she kept the sweet smiles going and hoped she had genuinely got the American hooked. She knew the fresh ones needed to be dealt with carefully but also you needed to pounce. Delay and before you knew it they'd be hardened to the scene and know all the tricks. Despite his putrid smell of stale sweat, his clothes and shoes suggested he may have a few baht to his name. He looked better turned out than the usual *farang* guys and there could be potential here. Nonetheless, Ting wasn't fooled by his sweet talk. There were many *farang* '*bpaak waan*' in this town. They'd spend a night with a bar girl and imply they were different from the others. They'd claim they were after something real, something serious. Frequently she'd never hear from them again.

Pinky spun around the corner on a motorbike taxi and Ting jumped on the back, her head was starting to pound from too much alcohol but at least each drink was another few baht into her back pocket. In Bangkok bars of that nature, customers paid extra for a 'lady drink', a drink they bought for one of the girls working there. This included a small commission for the bargirl. Many first time punters were not even aware they paid more for these drinks.

The streets of Nana were starting to thin out, but would still be considered busy by the standards of most places. The motorbike driver sped around the corners too fast of course, but Ting managed to stop herself from vomiting. Ting lived in a one-room apartment with her friends Pinky and Mint, it was close to the area she worked, yet the rent was just 6,000 baht a month. A stone's throw away were high rise condos that rich expats paid in excess of 50,000 a month for. Mint had been picked up by a regular tonight, and Ting was pleased for her. She'd been having a hard time of things and tonight's guy was usually a good payer and he had no weird sexual kinks so it would be an easy case of going through the motions, faking a couple of orgasms and saying the right things.

At the age of 21, Ting had been living in Bangkok for nearly 3 years. She had been desperate to leave her small town life behind and with trepidation and full of excitement she had enrolled at Bangkok's

Ramkamhaeng University. Ramkamhaeng was famous in Thailand for having entry requirements that enabled any Thai citizen to study there and Ting was genuinely excited at the prospect. Her mother was worried about her only daughter moving to the big city but realised it was something Ting had to do. She had her middle brother, Tong, who lived in the city with his wife, as well as Pinky, an old school friend of her oldest brother, Tang. All accounts in the village suggested Pinky lived a successful life in the Big Mango.

Ting did indeed start studying on her Media Arts course at university and was enjoying it. She was making lots of new friends and beginning to explore the city. The realities of her difficult financial situation soon became an issue though. She had briefly found a job in a café working at night but the meagre wage was too insignificant to make a difference in her life. As she struggled through her first semester she got in touch with Pinky, at the time more out of boredom than anything else. She couldn't really afford to go out as often as her friends and was spending a lot of time by herself in her small room. Pinky had explained her own life to Ting and there planted the seed that led to the start of Ting's work in Bangkok's most infamous industry. Her initial plan was to find a decent enough guy who could afford to put her through university. This had soon turned to full-time work in one of Nana's bars.

They unlocked the door to the basic apartment, and added their shoes to the pile that stood by the door. High heels, flat heels, flip flops, reds and blues were haphazardly placed in a cupboard by the door. The room was scattered with clothes and make up, and the bed was simply a double mattress on the floor. If none of the girls had managed to hook a client then they had to share. Pinky put on the fan and lit a cigarette. Ting felt a deep melancholy for her friend, she looked up to Pinky and respected her, but at 34 Pinky was starting to drink in the last chance saloon. Money she had made over the years of working, and they'd been plenty of that, had been guzzled by supporting her daughter who lived back home with her grandmother, Pinky's mother.

Pinky was struggling to make ends meet and her age was starting to show. It wasn't meant to be like this; she had high hopes for a life with the father of her child and for a while they lived together and talked of marriage and a life back in Germany. His interest soon faded, and the realities of being married to a working girl kicked in. He went back to Germany to visit his family one Christmas and Pinky never heard from him again. The bastard didn't even leave her money for rent. Pinky returned to her village with her daughter to settle her in with her mother, and was back working the bars in Bangkok within a week.

Pinky wiped the makeup from her face and it was only then that the real Pinky appeared, the sad eyes, the beginnings of wrinkles on her face, but it wasn't just the physical Pinky that was revealed when her work 'costume' was off. Gone was the beaming smile that she had perfected over the years. Thoughts of a grim future were never far from her head, and if it wasn't the future that terrified her, well the past was even worse. The hundreds and hundreds of drunken men who had climbed on top of her and done what they wanted, a large number of whom were so deluded that they thought Pinky was enjoying it. Pinky could honestly say that in her 18 years of fucking for money, she'd probably enjoyed the experience with less than 5 clients, and they'd been well over 2,000, probably 3,000. She didn't ever count. She didn't want to know. She didn't want to remember.

As a teenager arriving in Bangkok, Pinky had been innocent and blissfully naïve. Her first encounters in the sex business were certainly not consensual. She had remembered feeling horrible. Used and dirty. She had also felt a deep shame and hoped her parents would never find out. As she hit her 20s she had convinced herself that she liked the life, the money and that she was in total control of what she was doing. She wasn't exploited she'd tell people. She'd made a career choice, was earning money, living a good life. As she moved into her 30s she had begun to see the delusional nature of that argument. It wasn't much of a life. She wished at times that she just did something calmer, quieter, more boring, even if that meant less money. Now it was too late. She had to focus on making the best of what she had.

FOUR

As the first sunlight of another Bangkok day sneaked its way through the curtains, Bob Lowe woke up and immediately felt the drenching of sweat on his pillow. His feeble fan spluttered around above his head, barely providing enough of a breeze to enable him to sleep. Lowe found that copious amounts of alcohol tended to help with that. He grabbed for his packet of cigarettes, only to find it was empty. He hurled it across his tiny studio flat and it clattered into the pile of pizza boxes resting on dirty clothes. At least there were no food scraps lying around, the rats saw to that. He had got used to living with rats, he rarely saw them but he was aware of their presence, he told himself it was a useful way to keep the floor tidy, of food scraps at least. He lived in constant fear of waking up to find a rat nibbling at his most delicate parts! Bob had wondered if this could become a recognised phobia. He had once met someone who claimed to suffer from arachibutyrophobia – the fear of peanut butter sticking to the roof of the mouth. Bob wanted to invent aratadickophobia, but wondered how to get it into the public consciousness. Mind you, a rat biting on his dick might be little different to some of the battered ageing hookers who had nibbled at it over his decade in Bangkok. Such as the time he found himself in bed with a hooker who began servicing American men during the Vietnam War, she was probably in her 60s and had a body to match not just her age but years of selling her body.

Bob Lowe hadn't done a day's work in well over a year. He inherited $50,000 from a virtually unknown uncle and in classic Lowe style he decided he didn't need to work anymore and told his boss where he could shove it. He was down to his last few thousand and the sudden realization of needing to find some sort of employment was starting to hit.

He splashed water on his face. It was slightly lukewarm, which was about as cold as it got in his filthy bathroom. The sink was surrounded by detritus, 2 or 3 virtually empty toothpaste tubes one which Lowe had cut open with a pair of scissors to try and extract the last tiny quantities of paste. His method was simple, he would wet the toothbrush and then rub it around the inside of the tube until it was coated with just enough of the minty substance.

The wall tiles were cracked and the mirror was so filthy that he had to wipe a small section just so he could get a clear view of his face. However, that was something Bob didn't like to do in the mornings; at 41 he had the face of a 50 year old farm worker and it wasn't going to get any better. The toilet was filthy, with streaks of shit so dried in that they were probably permanent. Lowe did once own a toilet brush and in his younger days he had used toilet cleaner, but the brush broke and he considered it an unnecessary expense. He even believed that powerful urinating was more effective than a toilet brush, but the reality proved quite different.

A cockroach scuttled back behind the toilet as Lowe tried to aim his morning piss toward the toilet bowl. He was hit with excruciating pain. A familiar pain for Bob and he knew he would have to find the few hundred baht he would need for a short course of amoxicillin. There were few doctors who could diagnose STDs and their treatment with the speed and skill of Bob Lowe, he knew a dose of the clap when he felt it. He reckoned in all his years in Thailand he'd got the clap about 10 or more times and he had even noticed that he'd had to change his treatment routine over the years, as some antibiotics had become less and less effective. Bob was meticulous in his research of STD treatments. He was constantly googling for details of the latest research papers. He had even once enquired at Chulalongkorn Medical School if he could join the medic undergrads for the unit on STD treatment!

While at first glance he was something of a stereotype, Bob Lowe was a much more complicated individual. He lived the life of a classic 'Nana-Dweller', entirely dominated by alcohol and paid for sexual encounters. Yet, unknown to most, he had an IQ of over 140 and in his 20s had been snapped up on the graduate recruitment circuit. He left one of the UK's top universities with a first-class honours degree in History and Politics and was considered to be destined for great things. There had always been the potential for alcohol to be his downfall, and so it had slowly proved correct. As a younger man he was able to function without any major issues. In fact the long hours working for a major investment bank in London initially suited Bob wonderfully. Drugs and alcohol were a staple of the young traders and Bob fitted in.

Bob's problem was two-fold – boredom and guilt. As a leftist student who ranted socialist ideals, he had become the worst sort of traitor, a cog in the capitalist wheel. Bob inherited his intelligence from his parents, but neither of them had sold their soul in the way their only son did. Both had spent their lives fighting for social justice and campaigning for change as active members of the British Labour Party.

Bob's mother wrote and edited for a range of grassroots left-wing publications and Bob's father was well-known in intellectual circles as a classic British socialist academic. He was often on news programmes prompting debate with his strong anti-capitalist agenda.

Simon and Adele Lowe were outwardly proud of their only son, but Bob knew inside they were disappointed with his decision to work in the banking sector. They were elated when he told them he was quitting the rat race to teach English in Bangkok, to give something back. He even began hinting at an interest in helping to tackle the inequality in the fast developing South East Asian country. Initially, Bob had thrown himself seriously and passionately at his teaching, but he soon found it as equally soulless as the corporate world. It *was* the corporate world! He found himself predominantly teaching rich kids, and teaching them how to use the future perfect tense would soon prove to be tiresome. However, the job was easy and Bob could happily drink every night and still be at work on time. Frequently his weekdays didn't start until 2pm, such was the nature of private language schools.

Across town, 'Mad' Susie Hoare was also waking up, late as usual. She looked in the mirror and was greeted by the usual horrors. Deep dark bags under the eyes, hair that would make a scarecrow blush, and unsightly red blotches over her face. She was 35 but could have easily passed for much older, and here she was living in a country where the people were renowned for their beauty and everlasting youth. What had her life become? She looked across at Tong, her work-shy husband who gave most of his money (Susie's money!) to help his bar-girl sister. Mad Susie did have something in common with many women here though, she wore a mask, albeit a flimsy one. She lived in a fantasy world where she was thriving and living a Thai-*Farang* dream with a loving husband and a great job. It wasn't always easy to keep up the pretence, especially when her domineering mother called from the UK. There were times when she just wanted to burst into tears and tell her that she had failed miserably, that her Thai dream had become a living nightmare.

Over the years Susie had become a pathological liar. It started with small white lies, usually to keep up the pretence of how good her life was. How happy she was with Tong. Slowly the lies became bigger and bigger, it had just crept up on her. Susie was no longer really aware of the bullshit that spewed from her misshapen mouth. It wasn't that she now believed her lies either, it was more that her lies were like an involuntary action and once they were out she had little consciousness of what had been said. Of course this meant that people were never taken in for very long, she was constantly contradicting herself, trapping herself in a complicated web of deceit. She told some people she was Marketing Director for some big Thai company at the same time as she had previously said she was in a coma after being shot 6 times. Her restaurant was blown up by terrorists, but on another day it was her hotel and mini-mart that was hit by the Bangkok-Romania Freedom Fighters; an otherwise unknown group of Eastern Europeans fighting for the rights of those Thais with Romany blood, only Mad Susie had ever heard of them.

She had little memory of the previous evening, lost in a haze of cheap whisky and cigarettes slumped on the side of a small Nana sub *soi*. In a momentary lucid moment she felt deep shame at the way she begged Bob Lowe to sleep with her, when she had stumbled by him drinking on the *soi* with two other men. Lowe tried to make a genuine excuse, but she could see the look of utter horror in his eyes. Lowe had been there once of course, one drunken night when he couldn't find a decent hooker for love nor money, he bumped into Mad Susie. The lethal blend of a heavily made up desperate Susie, the dark lights in the bar, and the 12 hour drinking session that Bob Lowe had been on, resulted in what Lowe later described as "6 minutes of ridiculous madness". As soon as Lowe entered that hotel room, and indeed Mad Susie herself, he knew he had to get out of there as quick as he could, Mad Susie smelt like she hadn't washed in days. Her heart sunk when Lowe shouted "KEEP THE

LIGHTS OFF", and she was sure she heard Lowe mutter "You're shagging Pinky, you're shagging Pinky" over and over like a 'keep it up' mantra. Susie felt even more humiliated when out of habit Lowe threw a 1,000 baht note on the bed as he dressed and left.

Susie knew she was really at something of a crossroads in her life. She could feel herself slowly descending into an ever deeper depressive state. Even the simple task of getting herself up in the morning was becoming increasingly challenging. She did have a job, a moderately paid English teaching post for which she had neither the enthusiasm or motivation to do well. Her teaching swayed from mediocre to inadequate and disinterested. At least she felt more contented when her mind slipped into the fantasy realm. The longer she could hold the grim reality away from the deeper reaches of her mind, the better. She splashed her face with water and slapped her cheeks a few times to both wake herself up and command herself to 'snap out of it'. Whatever 'it' was. She dragged her feet towards the shower and hoped that the relatively refreshing water would be like some Thai elixir. She knew she would probably perk up a bit later in the day when she was properly dosed with nicotine and caffeine. The mornings though were tough. Her makeup regime was taking longer as it took increasingly more effort to conceal the blotches, the lines, and the general haggard look. For Susie it was an endlessly repeating task, her own groundhog day nightmare. 'How can I go on like this?' she frequently asked herself.

Honeypuss House was something of a Bangkok

legend, opened in 1963 to cater for American servicemen on their R&R breaks. They had unsuccessfully tried to become a 'classy' hotel in the 1980s before settling on its current instalment; part cheap guesthouse and part brothel. On the ground floor was a small bar, and of course the women were available for purchase.

Up on the 3rd floor Scotty Marshall woke with a spring in his step. The aircon was spluttering and dripping giving a slightly uncomfortable humidity in the room. Scotty jumped out of bed and whistled as he moved to the bathroom, a Thai style wet room that made Scotty wonder if the really lazy hung-over residents would shower while sitting on the loo, certainly a time saving system. Marshall opted for his own time saving and pissed while under the shower. The relatively cold water gave him a bit of a shock at first, but he soon acclimatized and washed away the sweat, beer and cigarette smell of the previous night. He caught a glimpse of his gut in the mirror and tried to suck it in, but a gut that size couldn't be disguised. He found it hard to believe this was the same guy who was renowned for his muscular frame when he joined the US Army, but suddenly he didn't care. He had Ting. His mind had been working overdrive. Could he get a job in Bangkok? How much would he need to earn to support himself and Ting, and perhaps some little ones? How did a girl like Ting so pure and angelic end up in such a desperate place? It was unfathomable. He was excited but also nervous about being the first foreign guy Ting had ever had sex with. She had mentioned a Thai boyfriend she once had, but Scotty would surely be a more skilled lover. He was in love and there would be a natural tenderness when they first made love. He was concerned that Ting might think he was rushing things. He could tell that a girl as shy and innocent as Ting would be horrified at the prospect of carnal intimacy with a man she had barely met. Give it time Marshall old boy, he told himself.

He sat back on the bed and pondered, what did one buy for a Thai girl? Flowers? Jewellery? He would have to take advice, Ting was clearly a girl with a touch of class and he knew he had to be culturally sensitive. He would browse the book shop, and see if he could find a book on Thai culture. Maybe he could ask Hayes and Lowe, although he doubted whether those two had ever had the pleasure of meeting a member of the Thai upper classes like he had. Of course he couldn't be sure that Ting was an aristocratic sort but Scotty Marshall felt he was a pretty good judge of character; perceptive and on the ball, he could see Ting a mile off. Perhaps she was doing an experiment, like in the film Trading Places. You know, seeing how long she could survive in the world of the poor and desperate. He wondered if Ting's father was in politics or an important businessman. Then again, why did she ask for the 500 baht? Aha, Ting you little minx, a classic test! A gentleman would always help a fine young lady in distress and Ting was testing him. Touché Ting. Round two coming up!

Scotty walked out of Honeypuss House before 10am, but even at this time the sun was shining pretty strong. Within minutes large sweat patches had started to appear on his over-tight T-shirt and he was frantically wiping his forehead clear. He quickly found an air conditioned mall and searched around for a bookshop. There was a myriad of titles, gaudy covers of bar girls and prostitutes and the tales of the dumb-ass foreigners they had lured into their traps. 'Poor desperate fools' thought Scotty as he picked up a book 'Thai for Lovers,' and another about culture and working with Thais. He decided it would be inappropriate to buy Ting a gift just yet, Thais are a very shy people and he didn't want to embarrass such a delicate soul. He would present her with a wreath of jasmine flowers, he had heard this would be seen as a great show of respect. He was convinced that Ting would appreciate that much more than any item of cash value.

FIVE

Charles Wedderburn-Press was the sort of eccentric character one didn't often meet, even in Bangkok he was considered utterly bonkers. An agricultural expert in his 80s, who found himself in Thailand advising anyone and everyone on agricultural issues, with a particular leaning to cider production. Charles Wedderburn-Press was from upper class rural farming stock and was West Country through and through. His accent was so strong one could almost hear the clotted cream and cider in his mouth. In the case of the cider it was probably true. "Ciderisation" and "Ciderise the nation" were two of Wedderburn-Press's favourite catchphrases. Those two words had taken on a chilling significance in parts of *Isaan* where once poor rice farmers were now struggling apple growers and aspiring cider producers.

Charles had lived a fascinating life, and whilst

always something of an eccentric it was only in later years that his eccentricity had taken control. Like many, he had his own reasons for being in this part of the world and in fact Thailand was merely a stopping point on the way to bigger plans he had in Vietnam. He was on something of a pilgrimage to make sense of his own life.

He certainly had an engaging patter and soon after arriving in Thailand he began to explain to all and sundry that only through the development of a cider industry could Thailand's poor regions move up the development ladder. With no established local cider in the market place, Wedderburn-Press licked his lips at the 70 million or so potential cider drinkers. Soon after, "Humpy Smack" was launched, the cider that Charles claimed made men more virulent and attractive, and women easier to convince of that fact. Cider, he claimed could beat any disease from cancer to crones disease to pubic lice. A court injunction in the UK prevented him from being within 100m of a hospital, unless he was a patient. He had spent 3 years vociferously campaigning for cider to be provided with every meal in every hospital in Britain.

Charles sat down at a local bar and began to go through his usual patter.

"Pint of Humpy Smack please my darling", he winked at the waitress as he ordered.

"You name Smack? You? What?" the perplexed waitress in her tight green dress with the logo of a popular beer written down the side, replied.

"Don't be silly sweet lips, I needs me a pint of Humpy Smack Cider."

"No hab."

"You don't have Humpy Smack, dear me I

thought this was a bar. Well just give me any local Thai Cider."

Charles knew what was coming next and sure enough she delivered the line with an assuredness that only comes from regular usage

"You wait jus a momen please.".

Out came the manageress, a stern woman in her 50s. "You mister, we no have Cider, no one like. You drink beer".

"You don't have Cider....Stone me crows...." Wedderburn-Press continued his routine that went into a feebly ineffective sales patter and was beginning to irritate Bob Lowe and Alf Hayes who were settling down for an afternoon drinking session.

"What is it about Thailand that attracts these losers" said Lowe, blissfully unaware of the irony.

He thumped his chest a few times, to kick start the system. Lowe suffered from terrible stomach cramps and indigestion and was forever banging his chest in an attempt to, well no one quite knew what he was attempting to do.

Hayes gave a wry smile and nodded towards Lowe.

"Bob, easy tiger you'll give yourself a hernia. I got just the thing for you."

Hayes was known throughout the seedy streets of Bangkok for being one of the only people addicted to antacids, 'magic yellows' was what he called the little yellow tablets that he always had stuffed into every pocket.

"Go on then Alf, give us a magic yellow" sneered Lowe.

Hayes grinned from ear to ear "don't have any sunshine." Lowe lifted his head from the table in utter horror and just a whiff of panic. If Hayes didn't have any magic yellows then the whole order of the world was being over-turned. Lowe's booze addled mind starting working in paranoid over-drive, and then a small packet of little orange pills landed by Lowe's pint.

"What the fuck are these?" garbled Lowe.

"These my dear drunk friend, are the alcoholic's dream. Say no to the searing pain of boozing on an empty stomach. These are magic yellows and then some. Got 'em from a mate of mine across the border in Laos. Orange is the new yellow my friend." Hayes had barely finished speaking when Bob Lowe popped an orange tablet and drained the dregs of his bottle of Thailand's cheapest local brew. They went back to sitting rather glum, without speaking.

They heard the unmistakable sound of a West Country accent.

"If evers I saw a pair in need of a pint of cider this be it." Charles extended his hand and said "Charles Wedderburn-Press is what they call me, professional cideriser. Wedderburn-Press by name Wedderburn-Press by nature." Hayes barely reacted, and Lowe looked up and said "What the fuck?"

"Well my friend it be clear to me that you look a little bit down in the dumps, and there be no better pick me up for a case of the blues than a nice cool glass of Thailand's own Humpy Smack Cider."
Lowe was now getting more perplexed.

"What are you talking about? I can't drink cider, I shouldn't even be drinking these beers. I'm on antibiotics, and I'm just here to chew the fat with my mate Alf." Lowe looked around to wave towards Hayes but the canny cockney had done one of his fleet footed disappearing acts.

"Anti-biotics you say? What be the problem… Alf? Did you say it was?" Charles was getting excited the topic was getting into his perceived and believed field of expertise.

"It's Bob actually, Bob Lowe. And if you must fucking know I've got a dose of the fucking clap, yet a fucking again, so go on fuck off."

"This could be your lucky day Bob. Did you know that cider has been proven in tests undertaken by my good self to speed up the metabolic and catalytic process of almost all antibiotics. Furthermore, Cider's known antiseptic properties will begin to work to fight those bacterial demons inside." Wedderburn-Press sometimes got lost in his own web of bullshit, but he was flowing well today.

"What's that mean in English?" Groaned Lowe.

"It means sir that when you piss it out it'll take the dose of the clap with it. Cider Therapy is used by many respected doctors I know. CIDERISE THE NATION!"

Lowe thumped the table and roared at the waitress "Two pints of Cider!"

"Humpy Smack Cider" added Wedderburn-Press.

With that the stern manager told them to leave and they stumbled out in search of the nearest Cider stockist.

SIX

Scotty Marshall strutted confidently down the *soi*, a new spring in his step. Gone was the hunched-over walk of the bedraggled depressed man. This was the majestic walk of a man in love. Yes, the belly couldn't be contained but Scotty felt ten years younger. When he saw Ting sitting on a stool outside the bar, he held the jasmine flower wreath behind his back. He didn't want to spoil the surprise. He knew Ting would be impressed that he'd gone for something classy and not some tacky materialistic gift.

"Ting, my darling you're looking mighty fine today." Ting looked slightly shocked, and then composed herself

"*Khun* Steve, I miss you very much."
So sweet that she can't pronounce my name thought Marshall, but he almost felt his legs give way at the idea that Ting was already missing him. This was

unprecedented.

"My sweet Ting, I have thought long and hard about a suitable gift for you." Ting's eyes lit up as he pulled an iPhone out of his pocket.

"I almost called my new friends Bob Lowe and Alf Hayes, but they probably have never met a girl as fine as you." Marshall put the jasmine flowers into Ting's hands and she looked visibly stunned. Marshall hadn't realised it would have quite this impact.

"Oh tank you, you very hansome, I go see my friend. Just a momen." Ting stormed inside the bar and sought out Pinky.

"You're not going to fucking believe this, Pinky. Where are you?"
Pinky walked in from the back adjusting her bra and dress, a middle aged skinny guy followed. She raised her eyebrows at Ting and Ting gave a knowing smile.
"What's up Ting?"
Ting hurled the jasmine flowers onto the bar, "that fat old American bastard, that's what. I wasted hours with him last night, and so far all I've got is a few baht from the lady drinks and these bloody flowers. I've just about had it with this game."
Pinky had been through this routine many times before with her protégé.

"The long game Ting, what have I told you about the long game. You are doing fine. That guy is prime meat, with a lot of fat to be trimmed. He hasn't got a clue, he is a freshly picked *farang* moron from the top of the pile of *farang* morons." Pinky had seen many like him, and many times Pinky had come close to 'The One', the route out of this hell-hole and these vile men.

Ting composed herself and dabbed her eyes with

water, and then went back to where Scotty was rubbing his ample stomach, the spicy pork dish he'd eaten earlier was starting to take its toll and he was musing over the quality of the toilets in this bar.

"I sorry *Khun* Steve, I very happy," Ting began to turn on the waterworks, this was masterful stuff from Ting and Pinky gazed on proudly from inside the bar.

"Oh my sweet Ting, I knew you would like it," Scotty moved his sweaty fat arms towards her and pulled her in close. Ting's face squashed against his torso and became instantly damp with sweat as the putrid smell of stale body odour, cheap deodorant and old man's aftershave hit the back of her nose. This was fucking hideous thought Ting, fucking long game. You'd better not be wrong on this Pinky.

"Tonight I take you to dinner, very nice restaurant." Marshall had only been in town a few days and already he was talking in pigeon English. It was hardly a wonder that the girls of Thailand spoke such poor English when the city was littered with native speakers who refused to use accurate grammar or tenses.

"Oh, that very good. I so happy go eat rice with you," Ting tried to show enthusiasm.

"Atta girl, I will pick you up here at 7pm, wear something smart and sexy."

Marshall could feel his dick begin to rise in his trousers. It had been a long time and already he was wondering what kind of lover Ting would be. He quickly tried to get his mind off the topic, to avoid Ting seeing the bulge in his khakis.

Oh god, here we go, yep there it is, thought Ting as she saw the trademark movement in his groin area. She suddenly felt sick at the prospect. How the hell was she going to lie there and let this vile specimen do his thing. She'd been with some lowlifes in her time, but the smell, oh god the smell of this one. She would need to speak to Pinky about getting some more of those red tablets or white crystals that make everything seem good, and she consoled herself with the thought that at least this guy wouldn't be able to last for long. But what if he was one of those guys? So old that he wasn't able to finish the job. She remembered the story Pinky told about the 60 year-old who was banging away at her for hours. Just couldn't complete the job, they were both bored and eventually his member shrivelled and he sobbed in the corner. Pinky was a skilled performer though, she hugged him and told him how good it was, and how he was just very tired and that they would try again next day, no charge. Pinky got a big tip that night and made sure she never saw that old creep again.

Marshall had a few hours to find a classy restaurant that would suit a girl of Ting's calibre. He popped back to the bookshop in the mall and started to look through a restaurant guide. The pictures helped, what he needed was white table cloths and smartly dressed waiters. Something with a bit of style.

He gave Bob Lowe a call. He had very kindly given Scott his number when they had met the other night. Marshall felt that Bob was aware he could learn a lot from a chap like Scott. Perhaps he wanted to know how to meet his very own Ting, mused Marshall.

"Is that Bob?" Marshall cheerily inquired.

"Yeh, what of it?" Lowe sounded typically grumpy.

"Bob! Good to speak to you. It's Scotty Marshall, and I need your advice."

"Scotty, who? Is this some sort of joke?" Lowe was genuinely confused.

Marshall chuckled.

"I love that British humour. Scotty Marshall you met me down Nana when I was lost the other night, you were with Alf Hayes."

"Oh yeh of course mate, what can I do for you?" Lowe was stalling, hoping that he would eventually remember.

"Well I am taking the delectable Ting out for dinner tonight, and I wondered if you knew of a place with a bit of style and class in this area."

"Aha. A dinner date with a bar girl…..well if I know girls like Ting then what you want is good and cheap *Isaan* food. There's a fantastic street stall near to the top of *Soi* 1 that does amazing grilled chicken and *som tam*, trust me she'll love it."

They continued to chat briefly and Marshall soon realised that Bob was not going to be able to provide him with the information he needed.

I must have sighed. Poor Bob, thinking of one of the cheap girls that he must date. Ting would simply refuse to sit outside on the street and eat food prepared in such surroundings. How could Bob be so clueless? I explained to him that while I am sure they do prepare good food in these places, I was looking for something classy and expensive. White table-cloths, fine wine, 2000 baht a head or something along those lines.

Lowe bellowed out a chesty laugh that then turned into a desperate coughing fit, it was some moment before he managed to speak again. "Then I'm afraid you've called the wrong chap old bean. 2,000 baht!? I wouldn't waste two fucks on a meal!" Lowe informed me.

I must admit to feeling saddened by his crassness. I must

introduce him to my beloved Ting. I must help this man to see a different side to Thailand. Perhaps this is all part of some greater plan for me? To meet the love of my life and to help this poor Bob Lowe. Is this why I am here?

My Dear sweet Ting,

One day, when we are married I hope to show you these letters. So you will see that I knew. I knew when we first met Ting. Perhaps you are doing the same? Perhaps right now as you get ready for our date tonight you are writing in your own journal your thoughts of nervousness and trepidation? Don't be nervous Ting, I can feel it. This is meant to be. We are meant to be.

I can't quite believe that after just a few days in Thailand I have met someone like you. Can I be honest? I am slightly ashamed, but I think my friend sent me to that part of town for a sort of holiday fling, a brief romance. Who knew I would meet someone so intoxicating, so exciting. It was wonderful to see your reaction today when I gave you the wreath of flowers. You were so overcome with emotion you had to go inside. I saw you there chatting with your friend Pinky. No doubt you were worrying about how to react. Don't worry Ting, I didn't expect any gift from you. The gift of love is more than enough. I cannot wait until our date tonight, it will be amazing. I know it. I need to do a little more research to find a suitable restaurant. You'll laugh when you hear where my friend Bob suggested I take you.

See you soon sweet Ting,

Scotty M III

SEVEN

There was usually a slow build up in Nana's bars. The afternoons had a very sedate, almost laid-back pace. By early afternoon there would be a smattering of punters, having an afternoon beer, maybe some food. Some might want a bit of quick afternoon fun. Most of the girls wouldn't start their shifts until 5pm at the very earliest, some much later. The traditional view was that there wasn't much money to be made in the afternoons, but some of the girls did like the slower afternoon pace. Whilst potential business might be thin on the ground, there was also less competition as most of the girls, and especially the most highly sought after, skipped the afternoon sessions. By 7pm Nana was starting to get busy and within a few hours the nightlife would be heaving, right through until the early hours.

It was 5pm. Ting sat outside the bar, just into another shift. Whilst she could hardly claim to be excited, at least this night promised to have some variety. She may have found the American slightly disgusting but he was getting her out of the *soi* for a few hours. She'd be in a different environment and hopefully get a decent tip at the end of it. She was also beginning to think more positively about the whole thing, as Pinky had told her this could be the dream ticket. Though unlikely, she wondered if she might be able to string him along for quite a while without having to have sex with him. She had to play it well. Hit the right lines and this could be a decent cash cow for her.

She was due to be met by Marshall in a couple of hours, but still she had decided to start work in the late afternoon. It wasn't impossible she could make some money before 7pm, she could always be a little late for the American, if needs be. Two hours was a long time in Nana, a couple of lady drinks, or even a short-time client could easily be achieved in that time. Officially, 'short-time' usually meant you would go to a local 'hotel' with a punter for about an hour, but in reality it was very rare that they would use the full hour. She had often made 1500 baht from a 10-minute quickie.

In the distance she could see Alf Hayes shuffling down the *soi* towards her. She sighed a deep sigh and got ready to smile. His walk was really quite distinctive, an attempt at a confident swagger but it ended up more of a weird sway from side to side; his gut usually wobbling as he went. Alf Hayes tended to wear tight T-shirts, to show off his ample figure. As he walked down the *soi* he would wave and make 'friendly' comments to girls in the bars. "Lovely to see

ya Joy sweetie." "How ya doing, lets catch up soon."
"Oh do I miss that ass, Mook." He loved that feeling
of being important, which was exactly as he felt.

Hayes had given Ting a few thousand baht when
she most needed it and he'd also sold her plenty of
cheapish *yaba* and *ya ice* over the last year or so. She
was grateful for that but this time she hoped he
wasn't coming her way. She didn't really have the
energy for him. He skipped down and approached her
table, and with a little flick of his head motioned her
inside. No luck today then she thought, she'd have to
deliver the goods. She sat down with Hayes at the
back of the bar, her eyes focused on his stomach
pressing against his tucked in t-shirt. Beads of sweat
were dripping down his forehead. He just opened his
palm enough to show Ting one little plastic bag and a
glimpse of the distinctive white crystals that had been
making her life worth living. This would certainly help
her get through her 'date' with the fat American.

"Ting my dear, no charge for this, but let's get
some more of your loan paid off."

She smiled and followed him up the little stairs to
one of the short-time rooms in the bar, a squalid bed
with sheets that were technically clean, but heavily
soiled. She took her clothes off and lay down on the
bed. Hayes' naked frame approached her, his hard
penis just visible beneath the rolls of fat. Ting handed
him a condom, Hayes chuckled "we won't be needing
that Ting my sweet." He fumbled around and
managed to clumsily insert his small member inside
Ting. Less than 5 minutes later he rolled off, satisfied.

"Top notch Ting, top notch. I think you are
getting better with practice."

"Thanks you mister Alf, you very sexy man. Feel

so good." Ting wondered why she bothered with the half-hearted compliments, Hayes wasn't interested. He gave her a smug smile and before she knew it he was dressed and on the way back down the rickety old stairs, to meet Bob Lowe for a few beers.

Bob and Alf sat and discussed some of the details of a business deal that Alf had offered Bob a few weeks earlier on just such a night, drinking down Nana. Truth was, most nights were just such nights......

"I've got a little business proposal for you Bob, I've been thinking of something suitable for you, a good mate. I'm not going to use you as some sort of patsy."

Lowe looked up from his beer, "I ain't no patsy."

"No mate, but you've got the intelligence to know how to deal with a patsy. I've got Ting's dumb twat of a brother heading Burma way to bring me back some produce." Hayes was getting into full flow now as he saw Lowe begin to look up from his glass with interest.

"I figure he would benefit from a wise old head like yours, no-one at customs is going to question a young Thai nurse pushing his post-op patient in a wheelchair, are they?"

Lowe looked up, bemused and bewildered.

"Brilliant fucking plan Hayes, though I think you're forgetting something? I don't need a wheelchair and I don't have an operation planned! Sometimes you just don't think things through."

Hayes gave a sly smug grin, and then in a magically puzzled tone said "don't need a wheelchair? Are you mad Bobby Lowe? After a double knee replacement of course you would need a wheelchair."

Lowe let out a guttural laugh from deep within his chest, so deep that it soon became a wheezy smoker's cough. He took some time to compose himself, and spat a large glob of phlegm onto the pavement.

"And what makes you think I am that much of a mug Alf?"

"You're not a mug my dear Bob, you're someone who knows the value of five thousand pounds".

Lowe's face changed, eyes wide open, a million things going on in his brain. 'This could be just what I need to keep me going for the next year almost,' he thought to himself. He tried his best to look only moderately interested, but Hayes knew he had his man hooked. Bobby Lowe would sell his old nan if it could keep him in beer and hookers for a few months.

Hayes explained the deal to Lowe. It seemed ingenious and what made Lowe feel so flattered was that Hayes was offering him a 50:50 split, this was unheard of from Alf Hayes. Lowe straightened in his chair, finally the respect he deserved. Bob Lowe was stepping up.

The plan was that Bob would fly into Burma with Tong, Ting's brother, and would check straight into a 'clinic', a small facility that had been fitted out with various Russian bought operating theatre equipment. There Bob would have two state of the art titanium knees fitted, and here was the brilliant bit. Inside each knee would be jam packed with high quality Burmese made *ya ice*, or crystal methamphetamine for the scientists. Each knee would have a street value of 5,000 pounds and Lowe and Hayes would have a knee each. As soon as he got back to Bangkok, Lowe would check into another Alf Hayes clinic and have both knee replacements emptied of their product and re-fitted.

Lowe, as a semi-permanent drunk, never even questioned why Hayes would do all this for 5,000 pounds. If he had thought just a little bit he might have considered the cost of two return flights, visas, fees of the doctors, even these low quality clinics would have to cost *something*. Hayes was no fool, he would make sure that the wheelchair that Bob would be delivered from Burma back to Bangkok would have more of the valuable product stuffed into it's hollow tubes. The Burmese had assured Alf that he could wedge in at least 2kgs, with a street value of over 100,000 pounds. The hapless Lowe was the biggest patsy of them all, Hayes would meet him at the airport and express horror at the old wheelchair Bob was in, unveil a shiny new one and pass the old Burmese DIY model to his associate. Hayes was rather proud of this idea.

EIGHT

Ting was enduring a truly miserable evening with the rotund American whose sweat problem seemed to be getting out of control. He took her to a hi-so establishment where Ting could feel the glares of some of the wealthy customers.

The Lumpini Park Hotel was something of a Bangkok institution. The first genuine 5-star hotel to open in the city, it had a long history and was a staunch favourite of Bangkok's 'old-money' elites. The hotel invariably brought feelings of nostalgia to those who were wealthy and important enough to remember some of the fantastic events that had been hosted there over the years. The walls of the lobby were adorned with photographs of the great and the good who had stayed at the hotel. It was the 'go to' place for hi-so weddings and was frequently the venue for Royal gala evenings. Those foreign dignitaries and royals who knew their history still favoured the faded grandeur of the Lumpini Park Hotel (affectionately known simply as 'The Lumpini'), to the slicker modern opulence of the 5-star chain hotels that were becoming ubiquitous.

As was the way in these places the aircon was fierce, but it didn't seem to help Scotty Marshall III (he had gone into great detail to explain to Ting the III that was added after his name). The sweat was building up and some of the spicy dishes weren't helping him. Ting found herself focusing for a good few minutes on a bead of sweat as it grew on the yank's forehead and finally had enough weight to speed its way down the side of his face before dripping down onto the table. She felt repulsed but it certainly helped to create the impression that she was listening to the painful explanation of how it wasn't Scotty's grandfather who was Scott Marshall I, but his great grandfather. For reasons unknown to Ting Scotty thought it of fascination that the naming of the first son as Scott had skipped a generation, starting up again when Scott's dad was named and became Scotty Marshall II. She looked at his fork and daydreamed as to what would happen if she pushed his eye down onto it. She imagined that there would be an impromptu round of applause from the staff in the restaurant, she smiled at the thought.

"Aha, I thought you would find that tale amusing my dear Ting, it seems we are bang on the same wavelength. I feel something special starting here tonight." Marshall clicked his fingers at the waitress and loudly stated "get the lady any drink she wants from the menu, I'm off to assess the quality of the facilities." He laughed as he swaggered off to the loo.

Ting was starting to realise she would need to

consummate this relationship tonight. She figured Scott wasn't going to spend this amount of money on a meal at a fancy hotel unless he got something in return. She was grateful she had packed her little glass pipe and the small quantity of the special stuff that she had got from Alf Hayes. She had gone through this routine many times, back to a customer's hotel and regular trips to the toilet to 'freshen up', while she inhaled enough of the stuff to help her go through with the awful task she had to complete. She shuddered at the thought, but also knew that there would be a time when she was high enough, that she would start to feel relaxed and quite happy.

The evening dragged on, and eventually they were on their way back to Marshall's hotel. Ting was disappointed to see where they were heading, "Honeypuss House" and not to the Siam Palace Hotel that the American had implied he was staying in. It seems he meant he was staying down the road to the side of the Siam Palace Hotel. Ting's heart began to sink, the Siam Palace was one of the top hotels in the city, and priced accordingly, yet with Honeypuss House in her sights it seemed her hopes of landing a really wealthy client might be rapidly fading. She had noticed he winced at the restaurant bill and gave what, for a tourist, was a meagre tip.

After an uncomfortable ten minutes while Marshall showed his disgust at needing to sign Ting in and hand her ID to the hotel reception, they made their way up to his room. While Marshall tried to explain that Ting was a sweet innocent flower, Ting chatted with the receptionist – she had known Neung for years, about how slow business was for her this time of year. Marshall was totally oblivious that the two were chatting in Thai quite openly about her prostitution, thinking that Ting was trying to explain that she *wasn't* one of those girls. It is considered common practice in hotels and some apartments to make night guests register in this way. Usually the guest would give their ID card and retrieve it when they left. There had been so many instances of guests being robbed by the characters they had picked up, that this system was created. It tended to work well.

The door to Scott's room shut with a clunk; for Ting it was like a prison door being slammed for another night. She tried not to scowl when Marshall made some crude joke as he put the 'Do Not Disturb' sign up. Ting rushed to the bathroom, "I need to have shower and do make up, need litten bit time".

In the bathroom she carefully took the glass pipe out from her bag and put a little water inside. She turned the shower on full, and carefully transferred a small amount of the white crystals into the bowl of the pipe. She held the lighter underneath and had that magical feeling of anticipation as she saw the crystals melt and bubble and the smooth white smoke begin to rise. She waited, her friends had taught her to always let the first few puffs of smoke go, and then she flicked the lighter again. When she saw the smoke appear she inhaled deeply and saw the smoke rush through the pipe into the water, and within a few seconds she was slowly blowing it out from her lips. She felt the problems begin to lift and the world was already starting to seem like a better place. She took a few more hits and stepped into the shower. During the course of the evening Marshall was impressed with Ting's attention to hygiene, repeatedly going back to the bathroom with her little handbag. He was touched, thinking she wanted to be as clean as she could for her man. As the night moved on he noticed Ting becoming more and more relaxed and calm and happy in his company, she was talking much more and seemed so comfortable there. Once Marshall had finally fallen asleep Ting was able to take more of a focused effort on getting high and as the early signs of day were appearing outside she started to feel quite happy about life. She would soon wake Marshall, get her payment and head back to her home.

She gazed around the room and saw Marshall's wallet and small case open (he had insisted on showing her the picture of him with Scotty Marshall II and IV.) She moved towards it and felt a pang of excitement as she realized he had over 10,000 baht in his wallet. Now that would be a nice evening's work. She then nudged open the suitcase, taking great care not to wake him, he was snoring loudly but she didn't want to take any chances. There beneath his passport was a nice neat pile of US bills, she fanned them out, a mix of 50s, 20s, and 10s, and while she didn't waste time to count she knew this was the best night she had ever had. She quickly stuffed the loot in her bag and rushed out the hotel, handing Neung a few 1000 baht notes as she left. Neung had already ensured that the numbers and name he had entered into the hotel register were incorrect and she knew he could be trusted 100%. She left the hotel and texted Pinky to say she had a great result last night and would be heading back to the village for a few weeks, Pinky would smooth things over with the bar manager and all would be fine. Pinky was with a new client in Pattaya for the weekend and she knew that when she got back to her apartment in Bangkok Ting would have left some money for her under the hairspray. The girls always looked out for each other like this, and there would of course be enough to compensate the *mamasan* of the bar who would moan and bitch that she was a girl down.

NINE

Once Hayes had Bob fixated on the idea of the $5000 he would earn from the 'minor' surgery he would have in Burma, Alf knew he could begin to be a bit more flexible and creative with the plans. He had made cast iron assurances to Bob that he would be treated like a VIP, nice hotel, top service, a few days to see some sights, great food. They'd have to fly economy on the way out there but after the operation 'straight to first class', was how Hayes had explained it.

"Bob," he said. "It will be a wonderful experience. The operation will cause just a minimal discomfort. It'll be like a 5-star holiday. I'm almost tempted myself, but you know how it is, someone's gotta keep tabs on the streets here."

Bob was positively excited by the idea, he'd always dreamed of first class travel and 5-star hotels and this little arrangement with Hayes was going to finally provide him with the opportunity. The money would help him to get started again. In true Bob Lowe style he was already spending the money in his mind.

As the trip became imminent Bob had been regularly grilling Alf for the full details.

"You leave the planning to Alf", was the usual reply he got. Unfortunately Bob was so lacking in perceptive skills that he didn't realise Alf was trying to avoid getting into a conversation about the details for the simple reason that the details were rather more simplistic than Alf had previously implied. A day before departure the first clear signs of the truth began to emerge, as they sat on *Soi* Nana and drank their first beer of the night.

"Well, I have to admit Hayesie, I'm quite looking forward to this trip. Don Muang or Suvarnbhumi Airport mate?" Lowe casually asked.

"Oh yes, should be a good 'un Bob, you deserve it." Hayes replied in typically evasive fashion.

"So which one?" As Bob spoke a bead of sweat dripped off his forehead and just missed the neck of his beer as it splashed onto the table.

"Which what, Bob?" Hayes continued to buy himself any time he could.

"AIRPORT!"

Hayes chuckled, ready to inform Bob how naïve he was being.

"Get a taxi straight to Hualongpong railway station mate. Train is such a pleasant way to travel."

Bob looked bewildered and confused, not an unusual Bob Lowe expression admittedly, but this was a new level of confusion. Hayes tried to spin it as best he could. Airport security was much too tight, it was an unnecessary risk, he wasn't prepared to do anything that would risk his business associate and friend being caught.

For the first time Bob began to worry about this venture, but he was in too deep. He'd get an overnight train to Chiang Mai with Tong, where they would be met by a vehicle and travel overland across the border into Burma. The train tickets were the cheapest Alf could get. Again he tried to explain this was all about protecting Bob. Travelling first class was hardly inconspicuous.

"I am not prepared to take any risks for you Bob," Alf still had a very casual air as he spoke.

"You will just merge into the background. It's been fine-tuned with a toothcomb, come on don't tell me Bob Lowe is worried about this?"

This sort of reverse psychology worked as well with Bob Lowe as it did with toddlers, and Lowe spent the remainder of the evening declaring that of course he wasn't scared, he just wanted to check the details.

The following evening Bob met up with Tong at Bangkok's main train station. They battled onto the slow diesel train that would cover the distance to Chiang Mai in around ten hours. The train ride was uneventful, as it was overnight there was little to see, and Tong had no interest in communicating with Bob. He pretty much ignored Bob's attempts at small talk and almost as soon as they were on the train he rolled up a shirt from his bag and wedged it between his head and the window and slept, barely waking during the entire journey.

When Bob got off the train and saw the battered up old vehicle that was waiting to take him across the border, his heart sunk. It began to hit home, that he was heading to have a not insignificant operation arranged by a man who considered this sort of transport to be suitable. His sweat levels began to increase even further and after rattling along in a barely road-worthy van and stumbling out into an unknown Burmese town, he was soaked right through. He quickly realised there was no 5-star accommodation in this town and certainly no international standard medical clinic. In fact, he entered the operating theatre through a small store of the 'Mom and Pop' variety, selling all sorts of basic products from toothpaste to cheap biscuits, in an old dusty setting that looked like it was a throwback to British era Burma.

Bob was relieved to see that the makeshift operating theatre was at least a little cleaner than the shop and there waiting for him was Dr Brown. Although strictly speaking the 70 year-old was known as Mr Brown. Not for the reason that many top surgeons go by Mr and not Dr, but simply because he had been struck off by the American Medical Association some 20 years earlier and had been drifting around SE Asia ever since. He owed Alf Hayes a small favour, after some trouble he had got into trying to haggle the price of marijuana in a *Soi* 7 bar that Hayes frequented. This was payback time. Brown said little to Bob who was in a permanent daze and before he had time to do anything the ageing 'doctor' was administering an injection to begin the anaesthesia. The last words Lowe heard were "better get going, I get a bit tired and shaky in the afternoons."

Lowe woke in such deep pain that it took him a while to register where the pain actually was. He ached all over and he momentarily wondered whether the septuagenarian doctor had done him a back operation by mistake. Bob looked down and saw what appeared to be a bloody mess on both knees, which at least gave him some confirmation that he had been given the correct operation. He was too groggy to have noticed the relief in Brown's voice when he leapt from his chair exclaiming "he's awake!"

Within hours Brown had fled, leaving Bob with a mass of pills to take. Brown knew it would be hard to avoid infections in this non-sterile environment so he was sure to keep Lowe pumped full of antibiotics to cover all eventualities. The following day, in complete agony despite having high doses of morphine to go alongside the antibiotics, Lowe was bundled back into a van with both legs now in a rough plaster of paris, to take him back over the border. He was in and out of consciousness such was the agony, and Tong kept forcing more pills into his mouth if he began to make too much noise.

When they reached the border, the full extent of Hayes' genius was revealed. The Burmese border guards carefully observed the smelly Englishman stuffed on a wheelchair with both legs plastered and struggling to string two words together. They had a quick discussion and realised the best place for this guy was out of Burma and into Thailand, with Tong helping to oil the wheels with a generous contribution. So, not 12 hours from waking from his operation Bob was laid down on the back of a minivan groaning and beginning a torturous 14-hour journey back to Bangkok. Hayes had sensibly realised that it was best to avoid trying to get Lowe into a train.

In his lucid moments on that miserable road journey, where even the slightest bump in the road sent jarring pain through his body, Bob realised that the 3rd class train ride that begun the ordeal was the most luxurious aspect of the trip.

TEN

When Marshall awoke the glow he felt soon turned to confusion. On the face of it, yes it did appear that his sweet Ting had made off with his Thai baht and close to 1000 US dollars, but despite the logic slowly kicking in, a part of him still hoped and prayed there was some sort of explanation. By midday when he had finished feeling sorry for himself he stormed down to the bar where he had first met Ting. Pinky had already phoned *Khun* Jeab (the manager of the bar and *mamasan*) and explained the situation and despite her predictable protestations of irritation and annoyance she would of course go along with the girls, it was only 15 or so years she herself was one of them.

"Ting no here, she just drink here last week, she nothing to do with me." Marshall shouted and gesticulated and Jeab 'sympathised' with him. "Not my fault who you meet in this bar, many bad girl.

Ting not work here, she just drink. I not employ prostitutes, no no."

When the police arrived they appeared to be very stern with Jeab, and Jeab looked shocked and scared. She was something of an old hand at this, Police Sargent Apichit Wuttiwatana had been working this area for a few years. He was a good man with a lovely family and while the American was sitting with the junior officer, Jeab handed Apichit a few notes and invited him to pop in for a few beers after work one day in the coming week. They took a detailed statement from Marshall and ensured him they would do all they could to recover what he'd lost. Just another typical Saturday morning for the boys in brown.

I felt a panic that I hadn't felt since my days in Iraq when I was faced with a near certain death at the hands of Saddam's goons. I guess my time in the US Army had given me an instinctive ability to smell danger and instantly make an accurate assessment of a situation, but I have to admit with my brain affected by my love for Ting I had found it took me a few minutes to work out what had happened. I am ashamed to admit it, I momentarily considered the possibility that my darling Ting had stolen my money. I hated myself for it, and told myself I would make it up to Ting ten-fold when I found her. I was starting to build a picture of what had happened, it was clear that that coarse bar owner Jeab had spotted Ting as an unusual person to be in her low class bar, and had had her followed. The thug that followed her clearly broke into my hotel room and kidnapped Ting while stealing my money. No doubt they would contact Ting's family and ask for a huge ransom. I had to track them down, that was the only way to find Ting.

The police and the bar-owner were both stonewalling me and utterly confused. Jeab it seems thought I was accusing Ting of stealing from me, and the police were simply ignoring my angry claims that they must investigate the kidnapping of Ting. I spent hours at the police station, speaking with everyone I could and eventually getting a meeting with the chief of police. I can't explain the frustration when everyone around you misunderstands the enormity of what is happening.

The chief, whose name was a nonsensical array of consonants started to give a speech he must have delivered to many saps over the years, despite my red-faced anger that should have made it clear to him that this was a different case.

"Khun Marshall, I working this area many years. So sorry that we have many bad girls who behave in this way, and steal the money. Many of them are very poor and taking drug."

"I dare say many of them are, and I realise that must happen a lot," I pained to explain "but I am not talking about some two-bit hooker, I am talking about Ting, a girl of high class."

I could barely focus when he started to claim that Ting had been in this sort of situation before. Ting was a fairly common name and how stupid of the chief not to realise that. I am going to have to find her myself. She had mentioned that she comes from a small village close to a major town in Thailand's North East. She had mentioned a short bus ride to her village from the town, I am sure.

I went to the best bookshop in town and purchased the most detailed map I could. I circled Isaan, and then using Google Maps I printed a vast array of maps showing the biggest few towns and cities in the province and the surrounding villages. The printing costs in the internet café of this expensive mall were ludicrous, but I knew it was the best way to start. If it took me to my dying days I would rescue Ting from these kidnappers, but my only way of finding her was to find her family who would ultimately be contacted by the perps.

ELEVEN

The room was hardly what you'd imagine of a private medical clinic, but it was certainly a few notches up from the place in Burma. Bob looked around the room. The lilac curtains were heavily frayed and the bright Bangkok sunlight was edging its way into the room, providing a slightly hypnotic pattern on the bed that helped Bob to feel calm. He lifted his head and could see a door, slightly off its hinges that led to a basic bathroom. He could just see the toilet and was pleased to see that from this distance it seemed clean enough. He focused on some rather pleasant wooden furnishings and a surprisingly ornate door for what was obviously a cheap guesthouse. Bob felt a little more relaxed, it was then that the pain hit him, a stabbing excruciating pain in both knees. On his bedside table was water, some fruit and a range of painkillers alongside Bob's simple mobile phone. He grappled for it and phoned

Alf's number.

"Fuck me this is bad Alf," growled Lowe.

"Easy tiger, you're just coming round. Dr Pongsawan said the operation was a great success and you should make a full recovery."

Hayes was getting fed up with his patient now, the drugs were being sold the cash was coming in and he could do without the hassle of a whinging Lowe.

"Should?!" Lowe tried to bark, but it was the bark of a small poodle without the energy to so much as raise its head to a doorbell.

"Turn of phrase pal, take yourself a couple of those painkillers in the bottle with the pink top and you'll be up and around before you know it."

Hayes explained that the bucket on the right was provided to remove the hassle of trying to get up and hobble to the toilet and that a 'fully qualified nurse' would be along shortly.

Lowe popped two of the tablets into his mouth, and put his head back to the pillow. The heavy mix of painkiller and analgesic should put him back to sleep for a good few hours before Alf's latest bar girl visited to make sure the patient was comfortable.

Sometime later, Lowe did indeed feel a little better after Lon gave him the sort of medication that *Soi* Cowboy's girls were so famous for, and Lon came recommended as one of the best blow-job experts in town. For a moment Lowe almost forgot the agonising pain in both knees. It was over quick enough, Lon was thankful for that though she wasn't best pleased with the smell of the patient and the fact that he kept forcing both his hands on her head. Lon wasn't going to complain though, she owed Alf big time and this was a small price to pay for his helping her out of a difficult situation with the police.

The pain was easing though and remarkable as it may sound Dr Pongsawan had done an excellent job in the trying conditions. Lowe was now able to move around the room slowly with crutches, and he was hopeful that he would be back out in his Nana domain spending his 5,000 in no time. He began to circle the room, proudly showing Lon how nimble he was on his feet. Lon waited an hour, she had promised Alf that much. "I go now, so sorry. I like suck your dick so nice you good man." Lon tiredly got the usual patter out and it got a delusional grin from Lowe, "oh yeh I bet you did you little minx," he pinched Lon's ass as she hurriedly left the room.

Bob sat back in his bed and gobbled on some grapes. Life wasn't too bad, how many foreigners in Bangkok had two brand new knees, he pondered. They had to be an improvement Bob thought, he wasn't exactly well coordinated so he wondered if this made him some sort of bionic man. He imagined the possibilities, the next Bangkok Marathon and a sensational first time marathon winning run? He'd always fancied himself as a bit of a golfer – he'd won some drunken crazy golf events in his day. Could he make it to the PGA tour? Perhaps not, but the Senior Tour? He licked his lips and thought about Bob Lowe at the Senior Open Championships or some such extraordinary feat.

In Lowe's day dreams the opportunities were endless. He even thought up a story to explain the dodgy knees. Perhaps a terrible accident in which he'd saved someone's life, but everyone would be aware that he didn't want to talk about it and he obviously wouldn't appreciate any media intrusion. In the lunacy of Bob Lowe's mind he began to worry that when he was famous the press might dig into his past and find out about the drug deal in Burma.

The acute pain woke Bob from these glorious daydreams. Lon's unique nursing care could only do so much. He popped another double strength codeine pill and waited for the effects to kick in and offer him some relief. He would demand from Hayes that Lon was provided on a full time basis to aid with his recuperation. He fumbled with his old Nokia phone, his clumsy fingers frequently pushing the wrong buttons as Lowe cursed the device, before he finally activated the speed dial to connect him with Alf.

Initially he tried to sound chirpy "Alf buddy it's your partner in crime here, Bobby Lowe." Hayes let out a sort of cross between a frustrated groan and a pally chuckle. "Not got time to talk Bob, hope you are busy planning how you will spend that 5k?"

Hayes felt the need to remind Lowe of the 'small fortune' he'd made from their arrangement in an attempt to make him feel guilty for his continued moaning about those fucking knees. Alf was trying to keep patient but his Aunt Sandra back in the UK had fully recovered pretty fast from her knee operation and she was a woman in her 60s. He had to bite his tongue on numerous occasions not to inform Lowe of this.

"I'm still in a lot of pain Alf, I can't cope by myself like this. I'm worried I'll have a fall. Of course some more time spent with the delightful Lon would help…"

"A lass like Lon don't come cheap Bob, remember we did a 50:50 deal on this buddy, why should I be forking out…"

"I've had a double knee replacement, twice, Alf. I'm in fucking agony here and not even in a hospital" Lowe roared. Hayes grimaced. "Ok ok Bob, leave it with me. I appreciate your role in this, we're partners now, as you say."

The quicker Hayes could get this out of the way the better. He had a stash of top quality Burmese *ya ice* hitting the streets and he needed to be ready to deal with the influx of cash as well as plan the next run to Burma. He felt he could start to enter the big time here and he didn't need amateurs like Bob Lowe holding him back.

He texted Lon and requested her presence at his small 'spare' apartment on Sukhumvit 22. Hayes was always careful to keep the shady side of his life totally separate from the attempt at respectability he ran from his slightly smarter address in Ekamai. This small studio apartment served as his residence for the seedier aspects of his life. He let Lon in and patted her tight ass as she put her bag down on the bed.

"Mr Alf, your friend he smell and I no like." Lon flashed one of her legendary angry looks at Hayes. This served only to anger the stocky Brit.

"After all I've done for you. Get down on your fucking knees you ungrateful bitch."
He roughly pushed Lon's head down and unzipped his trousers. She was a feisty one for sure, but Hayes liked that and he certainly wasn't going to let that stop him getting one of the best blow jobs in town. She quickly got to business.

"There's a good girl. Oh you're still the best and don't let anyone tell you otherwise Lon." He quickly finished and with both hands he held Lon's head to ensure there was no mess. She sat back on the bed as he zipped and tidied himself up.

"Now Lon my sweet, I know what Bobby Lowe's like, of course I do, but this is business darling and it could prove very profitable for you." He rubbed his fingers so she was in no doubt what he was talking about. Lon listened intently. Alf had been a good source of income over the years and when she had sold drugs to a client there was always a little bit extra for her too.

"Bob's in pain. He needs to be cared for, and he's smitten with that tongue of yours. He's also just come into a bit of money which might interest you." He gestured again with his fingers, to further emphasise this point.

"He rich man?" Lon got straight to the point.
Hayes explained that Bob could be a good short-term cash flow for her, a few months max. She respected his honesty, he made no attempt to claim Bob had endless riches.

A deal was struck. For 10,000 baht a week she would be Bob's full time nurse, providing whatever Bob required. A month would be enough for Lowe to be back on his feet and should give Lon ample time to more than double her payment through careful manipulating of the hapless sap that was Bob Lowe.

Hayes rang Lowe with the good news. "You must have made quite an impression on Lon, she jumped at the chance to spend more time with you."

"Aha! When you blow a bit of Bobby Lowe...." Bob tailed off, not knowing how to finish this inspired quote. He had a contented grin as he considered again just how things were starting to turn around for him. Could Lon be the one to make an honest man of him? Could she be the one who stopped him endlessly thinking of Pinky. 'Pinky,' he muttered as he fell into a painkiller induced sleep.

Alf leaned back in his chair and patted his bulbous gut as he watched the beginnings of another evening on *Soi* Nana. It was 7pm and he had been at his favourite vantage point for just over an hour. He had a satisfied grin on his face, he couldn't quite believe how well his plan with Lowe had gone. He'd persuaded a guy to undergo two double knee replacements in the space of a week, and made a fortune in the process.

Alf Hayes usually began his evening routine in the relative calm respectability of 'Shooters' where he'd sit on a tall chair facing the busy road and contemplate his evenings plans. In Alf's world this was very much 'Point A'. 'Point B' tended to be some form of debauchery; a live sex show, soapy massage, or gang bang with 2 or 3 of his favourite Bangkok girls. The excitement was the journey from A to B, which varied according to a complex equation of Alf's mood, the beer prices and offers in certain bars, and any friends or acquaintances who were out and about and in the 'Hayes zone'. Of course things weren't always straight forward and sometimes Hayes had to employ his cunning and remarkable local knowledge. Fortunately Alf had a number of the boys in brown (albeit relatively low ranking officers) in his contact list and in the event of any emergency they could be relied upon. This was just such an emergency, most of the bars in town were not selling alcohol due to a national holiday, but a couple of well-placed calls found Alf in a secret drinking hole away from prying eyes above a convenience store on Sukhumvit *Soi* 22. It was there that Alf wound up sitting just 5 feet away from

Valeriy Dublachenko.

Valeriy could smell these guys a mile off. In the case of Alf Hayes, pretty much literally. The stench of fresh sweat mixed with stale sweat which had been masked with cheap (possibly fake?) aftershave was enough to trigger his gag reflex. Valeriy was highly skilled in communicating with all sorts of people, including the likes of Alf Hayes. He saw it as an amusing, sometimes cruel irony, that in order to live his life of millionaire drug kingpin he had to involve himself with utter scum like Hayes.

It had always amused Valeriy the way Russian criminals were portrayed in movies and the media. His reality was really strikingly different. Valeriy was more akin to a businessman involved in the import and export of Thai crafts alongside his main official industry, property development. Even his drug cartel leadership involved a lot of paperwork, negotiations, strategic decisions, and recruitment. Any forays into Hollywood style gun shoot-outs were pretty rare, and regrettable. When Valeriy first began to dabble in the 'pharmaceutical' industry, it was to try and profit from exporting cheap cocaine and heroin from South East Asia to Europe and the USA. However, he soon noticed that 21st century Thailand with its increasing affluence was where the profit was at. Stereotypical street druggies were always to be found but it was the growing number of young middle to high income earners that had turned Valeriy's head. As with most economic aspects of the post-globalised world, Asia is the place to be. The world of drugs was no different. Valeriy soon abandoned his ideas to try and ship overseas, the risks and complications were endless.

There was serious money to be made right here in Bangkok.

Despite Valeriy's skills in communicating with people all the way down the food chain, the truth was he didn't have that much contact with the Alf Hayes' of this world. One of Valeriy's best defence mechanisms was that he really wasn't very well-known. He had no interest in perceptions of power, he just liked making money, or more accurately he enjoyed spending the money. Again, this was another way in which he differed from the stereotype. No-one feared the name Valeriy Dublachenko because no-one knew the name, and that meant the police didn't know the name either. He had seen a good many people fall foul of their own egos and blood thirsty desire to be known, and to be thought of as powerful. Valeriy also had a physical advantage in that he looked unthreatening, he was fairly muscular but his tall stature gave the impression of being a tad wiry. The epitome of a dull businessman.

It was within his senior management team where the names would begin to strike fear in people, but again only to a degree. They were slick enough operators to know that getting blood on one's suit was not good for business. Nat, and the 'Andreis' ran the day to day operations. One Thai and two Russians who were simply known as Andrei 1 and Andrei 2.

Alf spent 5 minutes trying to get eye-contact with the Russian sat just along the bar. Despite his pathetic lack of subtlety, attempted nods of the head and smiles, he was proving unsuccessful.

"Bloody good little place this, isn't it?" Alf's words had little impact on the desired target.

"Of course, I've known about it for years. Let's

just say some of Bangkok's policeman like to look out for old Alf." Hayes chuckled as he spoke.

"Da" snorted Valeriy, not sure what to make of this tubby red-faced character.

"Ah, Russian? What you drinking pal?" Alf didn't wait for a response and barked at the barman "another of whatever my Russian friend is drinking." Valeriy gracefully accepted the Londoner's offer and began to engage in small talk with this curious fellow.

TWELVE

Pinky had been listening to Scotty's ranting for around 30 minutes and while finding it quite hard to focus on his delusional fantasies, a plan was beginning to formulate in her mind. It was clear to Pinky that this guy was a moron almost beyond the point of belief. He was one of those guys who you meet occasionally, or hear tales of, but it was always hard to fathom that they actually existed.

The stories tended to get ludicrously embellished along the way, but there was often a thread of truth and sometimes more than a thread. She had once been at the centre of this, almost first hand. In her early days in Bangkok her closest friend was with a regular, elderly punter. They shared an enjoyable evening. He was a respectful, friendly and very polite Swedish gentleman who was enjoying his twilight years and was made to feel he was rolling them back. When *Khun* Nit left him on the Sunday he was so happy he gave her 5,000 baht. The next day Nit heard the rumour circling that he had died. What actually happened was that he had had a heart-attack and collapsed hitting his head on the coffee table, a tragic accident. He was found by the hotel's chambermaid when it was already too late. The story that started doing the rounds within a few days got more and more bizarre. Pinky heard from someone who claimed to have known a friend of Nit's that there was some weird blood fetish involved that had gone wrong and he bled out as he was robbed of all his belongings. At the time Pinky just chuckled to herself and preferred not to correct the story.

She needed to get her tactics right with Scotty Marshall and she knew it.

"I'm so worried Mr Scott." Pinky was fighting back the tears. "At first I thought maybe *Nong* Ting had just felt embarrassed and gone to stay with a friend…"

Scotty was already shaking his head to show how appalled he was at this suggestion.

"But she would have at least sent me a text" Pinky continued, warming to her role with a hint of panic now in her voice.

"Of course she would." Marshall barked. "A gentle sweet flower like Ting."

A sudden but understated intake of breath from Pinky had the desired effect on Scotty.

"What is it Pinky?" he snapped back.

"No it nothing…it.. no, not… it nothing" Pinky hesitatingly uttered with just the right amount of unease and confusion in her voice.

"What?! What Pinky?! Anything can help!" Marshall was now in full on panic.

Pinky looked at Marshall and began to spin the tale that could end up being extremely profitable for her. She wondered just how far this lowlife would go in the pursuit of his dreamlike notion of Ting. One of Pinky's many skills was her story telling, she had perfected it over years of dealing with these saps and she was eminently believable. She told Marshall all about Ting's family.

"Ting from a good family in Pak *Isaan*. They not like her come to Bangkok to make her life. They very traditional people."

Of course, Marshall thought. It fitted. Landed rural folk who expected Ting to become a good housewife and keep up the family name. Presumably they had a significant agricultural holding, like some of those vast commercial farms in the Mid-West USA.

"So give me the address Pinky, and I'll sort it out. I'll go and rescue her."

"No! *Khun* Scott, No!" a tearful Pinky exclaimed. "If they think Ting has *farang* friend that very bad for Ting, lose face for her family."

Pinky went on to explain that she suspected her old school friend who was Ting's older brother, Tang, may have arranged for her to be taken from Bangkok and forced to return to the family homestead in the small village in *Isaan*.

"My poor sweet Ting, she'll be expecting me to save her. We will have to take her by force. Show them who they are messing with."

Marshall seemed to be envisioning a third rate western movie where he rode into town on horseback and whisked his poor maiden back to safety.

Pinky contemplated her next move carefully.

"I alway get on well with Tang, I sure I can ask

him he let Ting go back Bangkok. I can't go there and not go to work, but if I call to him tonight I can start change his mind." Marshall began to furiously shake his head.

"No Pinky. You need to go there and see him face to face. Money's no object. I will pay every cent you need."

Pinky looked offended.

"I can't take your money Mr Scott…."

There followed twenty comical minutes in which Scotty Marshall desperately persuaded Pinky to accept 50,000 baht in cash plus any transport and accommodation costs, and take as long as it took to go up country and do what was needed.

Pinky sat back feeling satisfied; that had been easier than she expected. She texted Ting to tell her the good news, and they discussed how they could spin this one out. Pinky didn't want to get ahead of herself, she has seen too many false dawns over the years, but with careful planning she felt this could be the one. The pot of gold to sort out both their lives. She gave her young protégé some instructions and then began to map out their futures.

Bob was actually feeling a bit better on the day Lon swarmed into his makeshift clinic and insisted she was there to help him move back to his own apartment. He wondered if this may be the heady mix of codeine, alcohol and those sweet caffeinated drinks that had become such a staple in Thailand. He looked at Lon and grinned a big Bob Lowe grin.

"As I told Alf, when you blow a bit of Bobby Lowe." He laughed a long deep laugh that immediately turned into his usual smoker's cough, he pounded his chest. The jokes were lost on Lon who was still struggling to put on her skilled game face with this squalid individual.

"Why handsome man like you not have wife *Khun* Bob. I very shock." Lon tried her hardest to flash Bob a smile and she began to dig deep into her repertoire.

"Oh I see tiger. Young Lon likes herself a bit of the Lowe does she. Well just play your cards right and who knows." Bob was letting his mind wander into a new day dream. "You ever play golf Lon?"

"Golf! Not play but I like" Lon said seductively.

"Golf man very strong."

They hailed a cab and the driver immediately recognised a familiar scene, a dishevelled *farang* guy struggling down the *soi* with a young Thai girl at his side.

When Lon saw Bob's apartment for the first time she visibly wilted, her shoulders slumping. If any of her girlfriends needed proof of the poor *farang* barely making ends meet in Bangkok, then this was it. She couldn't accurately discern what that smell was. There was sweat, dirty clothes, cigarettes and what she thought was a forlorn attempt to mask it all with bleach or toilet cleaner.

"Home sweet home dear Lon. Be a love and give the place a quick clean and tidy. It needs a woman's touch."

She began to collect up some dirty laundry and threw it in what appeared to be a laundry basket. She opened the fridge and sighed when she saw half a carton of putrefying milk, a can of Leo beer and some tomato sauce sachets from a pizza delivery company.

She needed an instant pick me up and a clear sign that this could be worth her sticking around for.

"I need to go shopping for you Mr Bob." Lon gave him a hug and sensually nestled her head in his stomach.

"Let me buy you some food and clean up and then I give you some of Lon special medicine. You like I know already". She moved her hand down towards Bob's member and gave him just enough of a rub to get a reaction and leave him wanting more.

"Now you are talking the language of the Lowe! Now where did I put my wallet….."

Lon already produced it and helped Bob to grab 5 crisp 1000 baht bills, one of which went straight into her back pocket as soon as she left the apartment. A start she said to herself. A start.

THIRTEEN

For his trouble Tong got a free trip to Burma, though he didn't enjoy the company of that excruciating Englishman, and Alf had generously given him 10,000 baht in cash as well as 10g of Burmese made *ya ice* that was said to be top quality. He was a little uncomfortable with that quantity and he certainly wasn't a heavy user. He sold a few grams at a cheaper than usual rate to a mate and he gave a little to his sister Ting before stashing most in his special hiding place under a loose panel of his living room floor board. He kept about 2g out and texted one of his *farang* friends.

He had spent a few all night sessions round at the Aussie Tim's condo in Asok and alongside some good sex he got high for free – an arrangement he was very happy with. With Susie away for a couple of days he thought it'd be nice to have a bit of company.

Tong pondered what he was doing with his life.

When he had met Susie he had thought of himself as bisexual, well he convinced himself he was, as the novelty of having a *farang* woman appealed to him. For a while he tried to make it work, but he now started to wonder what the point of that was. Over time he began to resent Susie more and more and he was disgusted by any physical contact with her. The sight of her false huge grin and desperate attempt to create the impression of a loving couple made him hate her and pity her in equal measure. Yes Susie had effectively pushed him to be 100% gay and he now sought nothing but men. He still found something of a mystique over foreigners in town, but he didn't consider one worthy of a serious relationship. He had a dream of finding a nice suitable Thai guy and settling down to the sort of life that Susie pretended to have with him.

Tim was pleasantly surprised to receive Tong's text, not just that he had an invite to Tong's place (that had never happened before) but that Tong had his own supply of the stuff that they would need to keep going all night.

Tong began to make the necessary preparations. He was meticulous, all those teachers at school who said he had few skills should see him now. Over the years he had picked up many tips from his more experienced drug taking friends and now he was highly skilled. Scissors, tape and straws at the ready as he turned a simple glass perfume bottle into a new smoking apparatus, the perfume bottle he felt added a bit of class and style. He manipulated his standard lighter to provide just the right amount of flame, he could feel the excitement begin to build just in anticipation of that feeling. Tong laid out the paraphernalia on the coffee table, dimmed the lights and shut the blinds to ensure he had total privacy. Tim said he would be a few hours, which suited Tong just fine as it gave him time to get himself nice and relaxed and well in the mood. He used the spoon that he had skilfully shaped from a drinking straw and carefully placed a small pile of the white crystals into the little glass bowl. He set up his TV and laptop and chose one of his favourite porn movies, being sure to turn the sound on the TV right down. The last thing he wanted was for that nice middle-aged couple next door to be disturbed by the tell-tale grunts and moans of a poorly acted gay porn movie.

He lit a small candle, he found it much easier to have a flame permanently nearby, and using his modified lighter began to watch the crystals melt. He inhaled deeply, fascinated by the pure white smoke rushing through the bottle and then deep into his lungs. He calmly breathed out and could almost immediately feel the troubles wash away. A wonderful relaxation began to rush around his body and he lay back on his sofa with his pipe in hand and continued to let the magic happen.

Lon felt a little calmer with a 1000 baht bill in her pocket and having bought herself some nice lunch at one of her favourite street restaurants she then set about the supermarket to purchase some necessities for Bob. She would tell Bob she did all the shopping at the luxury mall "I know you luxury man need good thing" and that would help her siphon off another few hundred baht. She knew from Alf that Bob was not a path to riches so it was important she made it pay every time she could to boost her compensation.

Lon had been in this line of work for just over 5 years since arriving in Bangkok and she tried to send her parents between 10 and 15,000 per month. She usually managed to achieve this but it often meant she struggled with some of the basic things in life. Even living a simple life in Bangkok was not cheap and living alone in an apartment at 6,500 per month was relatively expensive. She preferred the peace of living by herself (on the evenings when she was not with a customer) and she liked the proximity to work. She also felt comfortable enough to bring customers back to her place, it screamed of being poor but also of having some pride and standards. It suited her well. By and large she enjoyed her life, she had a great bunch of friends all in the same line of work and aside from the occasional drunken argument there was a strong bond and camaraderie between them. She had toyed with freelance work but she preferred the tiny bit of security that came from employment with *Khun* Jeab and on a bad month she knew a friend would help her out. If she really was desperate there was always Alf.

She took a deep breath and walked back into the apartment.

"Mr Bob, I miss you, You miss me?" she said with her best happy smile.

"You're about to find out." Bob was spread-eagled on the sofa with his hand massaging his crotch. "We've both been missing you all morning my love." He motioned her over and she got straight down to work. At least he still smelt relatively clean, she had helped him shower before she left, and she found this aspect of her life relatively hassle free. She knew she was good, the punters kept telling her, and she had mastered the art of sucking away on a hard cock while keeping her mind on the more mundane aspects of life. She pondered a trip back to see her family after her duties with Bob had ended. Bob was making all the right noises but this was taking a bit longer than she had hoped. "Easy sweet lips, you don't want it over too quick" squealed an excited Lowe. Lon went for it even more.

"Haha when you blow a bit of Bobby Lowe….."
Why does he keep saying this thought Lon? She wondered if it was the first signs of old age decline. She could feel things were coming to an end as Bob put his hands on her head to signify the inevitable.

"There you go, taste a bit of Bobby Lowe, ahhh…..". She wiped her mouth and said mechanically

"I like you so much you very good man. Not same other *farang*." Bob smiled, yep he thought. She's hooked on the Lowe!

FOURTEEN

Ting's family lived in a small village just outside of Nong Khai in Thailand's far North East. It was an idyllic area, two small houses that had been built in and around the family farm and set far back from the road, linked only by a narrow track. The work was hard but Ting's father had insisted on a diverse range of crops which served them well. It not only helped the family to cope with price fluctuations, but it also led to a more interesting and varied working life. He would often enquire of friends, many of whom only farmed rice, why they didn't get bored.

Ting was always pleased to be back at home. She pondered the irony; as a youngster she longed for the life of a big city and now she lived for these quiet moments back with her family in Nong Khai. She had treated herself to a taxi all the way home from Nong Khai's bus station, and having not told her mother she was coming she was always excited to see the look of joy on her face.

Ting sat back and took a sip of her tea and looked at her mother who had a contented grin. She worried about Ting in the city, even though her brother had promised to keep an eye on her, and she was so happy to have her home. She urged her to stay back in the village and she could tell that Ting was contemplating it. She didn't want to pry but she knew that her daughter had something on her mind.

Pinky had been in regular contact and told Ting all about the crazy American. Ting found it hard to believe that this was really happening, she had only just met the guy and had made little effort with him. She had barely even put on a false smile or dropped in any of the classic bar girl phrases. She assumed it was obvious she looked a bit miserable in the restaurant, she almost felt sorry for him. Then she remembered how he'd rolled onto her with barely even a cursory inquiry as to whether she was keen, and of course there was his absurd presumptuousness that she could possibly have developed any strong feeling for him over the course of a couple of evenings.

She looked around the home and pondered whether life there could actually be pretty good, even if Pinky's plans did not come off. Her mother, Nam, was a hard worker. She had to be after her husband had died while Ting was still at school. Nam had managed the family plot where they grew rice, tobacco and had fruit as well as rubber trees, with the help of her eldest son, Tang. She had grown concerned about the future of tobacco as more and more people seemed to be turned off smoking. Rubber was also a concern, prices were low these days and she had even given thought to abandoning that element of the farm and extending the fruit fields. Tang lived with his wife and daughter in the small neighbouring house on the plot and although he worked as a mechanic in Nong Khai he still felt his duty to the family and spent much of his spare time helping on the farm.

He missed his sister and brother and longed for a time when Tang, Tong and Ting would all be together again in the village. He'd told them both that the space and money could easily be made available to build another small house on the family land. Ting smiled whenever he mentioned this and thought about what could be. She had complete trust in Pinky and would do exactly as she recommended. Pinky had known enough of these men over the years and Ting had seen first-hand just how skilful she was at working them.

Pinky called Marshall having carefully prepared her next move.

"*Khun* Scott. I'm right, Tang said that Ting is back home. I spoke with her earlier. She so sorry. Her brother take her and say she must stay in the village."

Marshall began to weep with desperate and anguished pain.

"My sweet Ting. Is she ok? Did you tell her how much I love her?" Pinky might have found this hard to believe had she not seen it so many times before.

"Yes she told her family that she loves American man. They not know if you good man."

Marshall felt a shiver of excitement, he'd finally had confirmation that what he felt for his darling Ting was mutual.

"But I AM good man." Marshall was already perfecting this ludicrous broken English.

"How I show them I good man Pinky?"

This was proving worryingly too easy and Pinky wondered whether this was yet another false dawn. There had been so many and despite how much she had toughened to the Bangkok scene over the years she still had that seed of hope deep within. She no longer dreamed of a perfect family life, she just wanted the best for her daughter and to be sure she had better opportunities in life than Pinky had. She wanted for nothing and was doing well in school but Pinky worried for the future if she wasn't able to continue fully supporting them.

FIFTEEN

Bob's latest mini windfall set him off on another daydream; at least this one had a hint of realism and tragically, possibility. He thought about the renaissance of a dream that theoretically became reality some years earlier. Namely, owning his own bar – Blow Bar, Bob Lowe, Blow, get it? Who could fail to get it he thought and who could fail to really get the appeal too.

Bangkok was saturated with such establishments of course and that is where Bob's shrewd business brain kicked in. On holiday in Luang Prabang – **The** Luang Prabang, UNESCO World Heritage centre of Laos culture, he became increasingly frustrated and angered at his inability to 'purchase' one of the waitresses. Some of the girls were positively offended by his suggestive overtures. 'What kind of backward place is this?' mused Lowe. He thought he'd finally found the right part of town when a rather comely maiden enticed him into a massage parlour. Bob metaphorically rubbed his hands with glee. Alas when he saw the teenage boy of around fifteen walk in to give him a strictly clothes on shoulder massage he realised he'd naively fallen for the old 'bait and switch' – that hadn't happened to him since his early days in Bangkok.

"Always confirm who is giving you the massage before you step foot in the establishment" Lowe would warn many newbies.

He went to bed frustrated and angry every night on that holiday, and then he had what he later described as his very own 'Eureka' moment. Something pinged in his brain, in Bob's own confused words 'this was like the apple falling into my bath.' Open your own bar! He got to work immediately, never had Bob been so focused and motivated by work. He persuaded his elderly parents to remortgage their home in Sussex and plunged about $50,000 into the most lunatic of ideas.

'I'll do to blowjobs what Starbucks did to coffee' was his mantra. He dreamt of a Blow Bar in every high street, he'd become a global campaigner for the legalisation of blowjob bars, a human rights hero. The logo left no doubt as to what the main business of the bar was, and he had got ahead of himself planning merchandise and add-on sales. He recruited 6 of *Isaan*'s finest girls and paid handsomely above and under the counter for their official employment in Laos. These would be his 'Blow Job Ambassadors', training the locals, and of course Lowe figured he could charge a premium for 'a bit of Thai'. The venture was, alas short-lived, no sooner had the bright neon lights lit up half of the Mekong River and the fliers enthusiastically handed out that he got a visit from the local constabulary.

Bob was utterly perplexed, but not unduly worried as he felt he knew exactly how to appeal to the police's desires. "This problem will all BLOW away" he chuckled out loud. He proudly showed the police his wooden and gold embossed special menu which included such gems as:

- Beer Lao and Blow Job
- 2 Beer Lao and Full Service

There was also a list of 'Bob's Special Packages', weekly specials that would allow 2 blows and 3 beers a day for a five-day spell. In the future he had planned loyalty cards, "Your 11th blow job is on us!" He was a man of the world and showed no prejudice. His other plans included an attempt to appeal to all. He planned to have men, lady boys, all sorts right there to deliver what was needed.

He was fined on the spot and ordered to shut with immediate effect. He desperately argued that it was all a bit of a joke, a play on words, no harm done. The sight of Lowe hurriedly back tracking was quite something. It worked though, after paying thousands of dollars in fines and bribes he reopened for a two-week spell, a truly dismal two weeks in which his total takings amounted to $16US. He spent most of his time trying to move away some annoying traveller types who took it upon themselves to warn tourists away. He would shout at them every night 'Go on, sling your hook, move it on. Get out of it!' The more amused they got the more incensed Lowe got.

This episode wasn't Bob's first brush with the law.

In his early fresh faced days in Thailand he'd marched to the police to explain he had been robbed. He explained his predicament with a bar girl to the bemused officer.

"We agreed 1000 baht for a fuck and a blow job and what resulted was what could only be described as a mediocre handjob." Bob managed to negotiate a bribe to the policeman to avoid being arrested for soliciting sex.

The Luang Prabang saga eventually reached a dismal conclusion. One evening he quietly ordered a taxi to drive him to Vientiane, from where he strolled over the bridge with a tear in his eye and back to Thailand. He promptly went to the first massage parlour he could find in Nong Khai and negotiated which girl he wanted. As he reached the point of climax he screamed out loud "THAILAND! I'm home again!"

He left behind in Laos 6 Thai girls for whom the locals fortunately had plenty of sympathy – victims of the hideous Bob Lowe. They closed the bar, and re-opened 6 months later with a cute Thai *Isaan* café which became a very successful Laos funded restaurant educating people in the close links between the cuisine of Laos and that of the *Isaan* region of Thailand.

Despite his spectacular failure, Bob put it all down to simple 'marketing problems' and a lack of research on his part. He vowed to re-open again in Thailand where his passion for blow jobs would be appreciated. After all, most great businessmen fail at the first attempt, Lowe had read that somewhere.

SIXTEEN

Pinky kept Scotty Marshall waiting, she had this carefully thought out and she called him with the right amount of seriousness in her voice. "I speak with Ting many times…"

"Ting! My sweet Ting!" cried Marshall. Pinky tried to keep her composure.

"She confuse, she in love and she not want to upset her family, her mother. They simple people. She not want you know she just normal poor farm girl, she think you not want that. Her family have no money they need Ting."

"Money?! Is this what this is all about Pinky?"
Pinky had to tread carefully here she knew this was not the right time and she did not want to lose her captive punter.

"No, no *Khun* Scott. Money not important to Ting. She want to help her family. Her family worried about *farang* man. Many bad *farang* in Bangkok."

Scotty Marshall III listened intently as Pinky did her best to explain the cultural issues at play here. With deft subtlety she dropped in, in passing and indirectly of course, the need for money and that money could indeed make a difference in the lives of Ting and her family.

She was sure Scott was able to read between the lines. Yes, of course Ting would love to set up home with him but she also wanted to stay with her family and what the family needed was some form of financial security. She hoped this was slowly dripping through and in the fullness of time Marshall would reach the only logical, sensible conclusion that a man in love, that a man in love with a woman he'd barely known for a week, could make.

She assured Scott not to give up. That she would do her best to convince Ting that being with Scott was the right move for her, that they could start a family, that she could be happy and have a wonderful future together. She could hear Marshall sobbing on the other end of the phone

"My Ting, my beautiful Ting!"

As soon as Pinky had hung up the phone Marshall began to think things through. 'No one gets anywhere without taking a risk' he repeated this to himself over and over. He pondered his whole life of safe choices, especially when it came to matters of the heart, and look where that had got him. No, he decided an enormous dramatic gesture to show Ting and her family how serious he was would be the only answer. 'You've got to task a risk in life Marshall damn it.'

He asked himself some tough, soul searching questions.

Do I love Ting?
Does Ting love me?
Is Ting genuine? (he felt guilty even thinking this)
Do I want to spend the rest of my life with Ting?

That's the difference between me and the losers out there, he thought, I am thinking things though carefully. The answer to all those questions was an emphatic yes! And despite being alone in the hotel room he punched the air and shouted YES! He tried to stay calm as he planned his future with Ting, but he was excited, damn was he excited.

Lon began to unpack the shopping back at Bob's hovel. Bob was apoplectic. "Shower gel! Shampoo! Hand wash! What are you playing at Lon? You are playing right into the hands of these evil multinationals who want you to think you need this. Good lord, you have a lot to learn dear girl. Stick with Bobby Lowe and get ready for an education."

Bob explained the 'Lowe System'! One bottle of toilet cleaner was a mere 50 baht (cheaper with some brands or buying in bulk), a fraction of the price Lon had paid for each of these items she had bought.

"Toilet cleaner! No! You not wash with that, it dangerous!" a bewildered Lon squealed.

"Indeed it is dear Lon, indeed it is. You have hit the nail smack bang on the head. It's too strong. Exactly what I thought many years ago before I unearthed the truth. Let me demonstrate."

He took an empty bottle of shower gel he had under the sink, the large pump action type, it looked as if he had owned it some years as it was smeared with layers of liquid dripped down the sides and it was dirty around the rim. Bob carefully unscrewed the lid and poured in some of his favourite alpine fresh toilet cleaner into it. Lon looked on utterly horrified.

"Yes Lon, I learnt the hard way that toiler cleaner is too strong for the skin and the hair, or at least neat toilet cleaner. I didn't just give up. I created the Lowe formula."

He went on to explain as he made up the bottle, 5 parts toilet cleaner, 1 part washing up liquid (to create a rich lather) and then fill the bottle with water (20 parts), and there it is. The ultimate shampoo, shower gel, conditioner, hand soap all in one! With this method, Lowe explained he could spend 200 baht a year on these toiletries.

"You've spent over 500 baht today alone on all these pointless potions and lotions. To think there are people who still pour this toilet cleaner down the toilet. What about the environment?"

Lowe had realised his environmental argument was a wonderful way for him to defend any of his most unpleasant of habits. If he limited his showers "we mustn't waste water, think about the farmers," when he ate rancid food from his fridge "what about the starving people?" or on another day "remember global warming."

Bob prattled on to Lon and explained how he had begun to write a book "Bob Lowe's Thrifty Bangkok Living" but he feared he might face repercussions from angry corporate types and the 'shower-gel mafia'. Bob wanted to explain to all that cooking oil should be changed twice a year, at the most. Bob's system was to simply keep the oil in the frying pan and take out the fried debris, or on occasion strain through a cotton muslin. He always kept the frying pan covered though, as he explained to Lon "health is paramount." Bob also asked Lon if she had noticed that many Thai people would eat their noodles on the *soi* and leave a large amount of perfectly good soup in the bowl. The quick thinking Lowe would pounce and pour the leftover soup into a flask for free sustenance. He opened his freezer to display to Lon an array of plastic containers all filled with left-over soup. Another secret of Lowe's was 'Bob's gourmet food walks'. He'd head to a few top supermarkets in town and fill himself up with the little tasters they offered; cheese, salami, bread, and the occasional new fruit drink were the mainstays. Bob's favourite trick was to consume a few pieces of cheese and mutter

"hmmm a tad too bitter for my liking."

"You stick with me girl and you will soon learn the tricks and how to increase your savings in no time." He shook his head while looking at Lon's purchases

"amateur hour."

A cursory glance of Bob's apartment did little to sell the idea of Bob's thrifty Bangkok living.

SEVENTEEN

"Keep your cool Scotty boy," Marshall said to himself after the phone call with Pinky. From what she had said to him he was carefully beginning to piece together a clear idea about Ting's family and the sort of people they were. He had been wrong to think they were aristocratic types, he mused, but he was right about them being proud and upstanding people. The longer he spent in Thailand the more he'd learnt about these women who worked in bars with the sole purpose of scamming some unsuspecting love-sick sap. This explained the attitude of the English pair he'd met that night in Bangkok. However, he was right about Ting, more right than he could ever imagine. This had now been confirmed by Pinky. He had to play this carefully and smoothly, it was all too clear that a crass offer of money would be rejected out of hand and he concluded would massively offend such proud people as Ting and her wonderfully rural family.

His father had witnessed some of that during his time in Vietnam and told countless stories of local people trying to get on with their day to day lives as his nation did all they could to rescue them from the depths of despair and depravity that was communism. Scott Marshall II was sure that those villagers were very appreciative of the US Army's attempts. He remembered distinctly one time as he was traipsing through an elderly farmer's rice paddy. Scotty Senior shrugged at the farmer as if to say "what can I do?" The farmer turned away and walked into his small house. He showed no aggression or animosity towards Marshall or the US Army, which Scotty II took as tacit support of US actions. Of course, the farmer couldn't make a public show of it.

Scotty had planned to visit Vietnam during this trip, in honour of his father and ponder what might have been for that poor tragic country. Scott's father always told his son that he was furious when the US withdrew, another 5-10 years could have broken the Vietcong he was sure of that.

He began to do his research, googling about moving to Thailand and about starting a business in Thailand, buying a house. He knew he needed to do extensive planning as it was quite a complicated business, the rules about foreigners owning land and such. He needed to be ready to activate a plan when the time was right. When a girl like Ting is on the market you don't hang about, you have to get in quick and see off the competition. He had some savings and he could cash in his pensions. He reckoned he could quickly get together $250,000 and be ready to start a new life with Ting in this wonderful country.

He needed her to know he was serious and he needed her to know she would be well supported by him, but without any vulgar display of wealth. He sent a few emails to his bank manager and a financial advisor he had previously used in the US, just quietly telling them of his plans to emigrate to Thailand to start a business and what he needed to do to free up all his capital as soon as possible.

He texted Pinky, using his words carefully.

'Pinky, I can wait for my dear Ting. I know Thailand is right for me so I'm looking into moving here and starting a business, maybe a restaurant – perhaps a good old American Burger joint.'

He wanted this to be passed on to Ting. He wondered if Ting would be dreaming of running such a place, dressed up in the Stars and Stripes. It could be called 'Ting's Place' or to show their true love 'Scotty and Ting's Burger Paradise'. He began to work out the menu in his mind, this was going to take Thais on a culinary adventure:

'The Sweet Ting' – a beautiful juicy burger with the sweetest chilli sauce and a slice of Thai pineapple. Then for him they would have 'The Big Yank' – a treble burger packed with cheese, bacon and jalapeno peppers with mayonnaise and ketchup. He could imagine how successful it would be. He pondered if the people in Ting's province had ever even seen a hamburger. He doubted it somehow and tried to imagine how proud the people would be seeing it run by one of their own. Ting would surely become something of a local celebrity. After all, how many Thai girls from rural *Isaan* landed themselves a genuine all American guy?

He woke from his day dream and continued with

his online research. Every so often he stumbled upon one of these websites with some dreadful tale of woe, a foreigner who found himself hooked up with a no good sort and getting conned out of all his money. In some circumstances even ending up murdered by a wife. There were tales of guys building property to live in with their wives and when it was all finished they were unceremoniously dumped, and with Thai law as it was they didn't own the land and didn't have a leg to stand on. Marshall shook his head in despair. He wondered how desperate and pathetic these people must be to get into that sort of situation. How could they not have seen what was happening to them? He felt very sorry for them, and supposed that some people are just so desperate to chase a dream that they lose all sense of reality. It was a shame, it really was.

Bob sprawled on his sofa, even he could begin to smell the body odour wafting from under his armpits. He was lying in a pool of sweat and beginning to stick to the cheap plastic faux leather sofa. His knees ached and he tried to reach for his codeine tablets. He grabbed at the selfie stick that he'd taken from Lon as a makeshift back, balls, and knees scratcher and tried desperately to swipe at the tablets. He only succeeded in knocking them to the floor.

"Lon!" he growled, 'Lon!"

"Why you shout me?!" snapped back Lon who was busy chatting with her friends online.

"I've dropped the pills, that fucking stick of yours is no fucking good."

Lon stomped over and picked up the small bottle of

pills, and handed them to Bob. He immediately fumbled at his boxer shorts and removed his shrunken cock with the instruction "I'm not the only one who needs the medicine, Lon honey."

Lon could barely hide her sigh, and she got down to business. After a few moments, with the desired effect evident in Bobby Lowe she paused and said

"after finish I go shopping, need new shoes."

"Ok my sweet lips" Bob mumbled impatiently and pointed Lon back to the job he wanted her to complete. Lon was in her element now, she skilfully teased and manipulated Bob's most sensitive parts.

"Maybe my lovely Bob and little… no Big Bob give me money help me buy nice sexy shoes….." She flicked her tongue and resulted in a desperate groan from Lowe.

"Anything for you love, especially if you do a good job of it."

'Never fails' thought Lon and she worked to complete the task as quickly as she could. She tried to keep her mind away from the dreadful stench of Lowe and went through the motions of focusing her mind on something else. Where would she go shopping? What type of shoes should she buy? Should she pick up some new clothes?

She finished in good time and near sprinted to the bathroom where she spent a full 5 minutes brushing her teeth and washing her face before spraying copious amounts of perfume to freshen herself up. She went back to Bob in the living room.

"Oh so nice like always *Khun* Bob." She went through the motions of lovingly stroking Bob's leg for what she deemed to be long enough.

"Ok now I go shopping."

"Ok sweet lips, let's get the Lowe's wallet." Lowe handed her 2000 baht. Lon did her best to look utterly shocked.

"2000 baht! Where I buy nice shoe for 2000 baht!?"

"Sorry Lon love, I'm out of cash, that's all I got on me."

"Oh Bob! That ok you nice man. I take your ATM card it ok. No problem."

Bob pondered and began to look a little stressed.

"Now now, I don't think we can be doing that sweetie."

Lon instantly began to turn on the waterworks, another of her great skills and began to go into an emotional rant. "I care you so much and you not care me same. You think I bad girl steal from you every time. I sad. I good girl. I like you much and maybe you not like me…" Lon continued to weep dramatically.

It never failed with an utter mug like Lowe.

"There there Lon, what was I thinking. Here's my card. 1-2-4-8. You be careful out there. 4000 will cover it?" Bob's question tailed off rather pathetically.

Lon snatched the card from Bob's grasp and couldn't get out of there quick enough. Bob felt a twang of concern but he let it pass. He was in no position to turn away the one person who was helping him through this situation and he figured a few thousand baht was a small price to pay for the care and attention Lon was giving him to ensure his rehabilitation was a full success.

Bob had needed the aid of a bar girl to help him rehabilitate some years previously when he broke a leg falling down a flight of stairs in *Soi* Cowboy after a notorious Christmas Challenge. On a quiet Christmas Eve, Bob had been out drinking with Alf Hayes. Alf had casually mentioned a friend from back home who had recently visited, a woman no less, who he claimed could out drink Bob Lowe. Bob was crestfallen and offended. The one thing that he clinged to, the one thing he had in life was his ability to drink alcohol. Deep in his subconscious he knew if he didn't have that, he had nothing. He looked up at Hayes and immediately settled his bill in the bar. On the way home he purchased a bottle of Baileys, a bottle of Vodka (raspberry infused), and one of Kahlua. He went to bed feeling rather depressed. He was meeting Alf again the following day at one of the British pubs for a traditional Xmas dinner, the deal included free flow beer. He'd show 'em. He repeated this over in his head as he eventually fell asleep.

His Christmas Day breakfast was a bowl of cereal. Only Lowe replaced the milk with Baileys. For fruit juice he downed copious amounts of the raspberry vodka and of course no breakfast would be complete without a morning coffee or two, for Bob this was Kahlua with a splash of milk added. He polished off the bottle of Baileys and much of the other two. He left his house grasping the Kahlua bottle to which he had added the remainder of the Vodka. An hour into dinner he threw up over the table and scolded the waitress for the 'dodgy turkey', whilst screaming "free flow beer, free fucking flow." He was forcibly evicted from the pub and he meandered his way down to *Soi* Cowboy. His state was such that he was moved on after 1 or 2 drinks in three separate bars (quite an achievement to be too drunk for *Soi* Cowboy). It was in that fourth bar that the first step downstairs to the bathroom proved to be beyond his coordination. It was 10 minutes before Pinky found him curled up in a foetal position and whimpering in pain. Hence begun his feeling that Pinky was an angel sent from some Thai deity to save him.

EIGHTEEN

Pinky went to see *Khun* Jeab in the early afternoon, a couple of days after her most recent exchange with Scotty Marshall.

"You back here to work *Nong* Pinky?" asked Jeab, straight to business.

Pinky explained that she had just come for a chat and some advice. On the surface Jeab was a hardened character but she had once been something of a mentor to Pinky, as Pinky was now to Ting. The torch of knowledge being passed on down the generations. When push came to shove Jeab would always be there for one of her loyal girls and Pinky was one of the most loyal she had ever known.

With no children of her own it had become Jeab's plan that Pinky take over her management position in the bar and take care of Jeab in her old age. That was the realist in Jeab, but of course she hoped that Pinky might find a calmer and easier route to happiness and security than dealing with Nana's dwellers 7 nights a week. She had become acutely aware that this odd yank, Scotty, could become Pinky's ticket out of Nana and Jeab couldn't help but realise there could be potential for her there too. Pinky would surely look after the one person who was always there for her in Bangkok.

Jeab listened intently to Pinky's explanation of the plans to date, nodding in agreement and approval of the accomplished way her younger charge was manipulating this loser. Jeab had filled Pinky in about the American's ludicrous visits to the bar when he thought Ting had been kidnapped and agreed that this man was ripe for picking. Jeab told Pinky her take on the matter

"You have to be brave and move fast. The quicker you are the more chance you have of real success." Jeab helped Pinky put together a solid plan of action.

Afternoons tended to be quiet in the bar. Jeab looked around, there were two guys in their 20s (Australians she thought) playing pool, and one older chap who was something of a regular sitting at the front looking out onto the *soi* with his bottle of Singha. A cockroach scuttled across the floor, much to Jeab's irritation, she took great pride in keeping her bar as clean and hygienic as possible, but in the semi-open air environment of *Soi* 4 it was impossible to be rid of these 6-legged beasts altogether. One of the Aussies kicked the roach out towards the entrance, just as the girl he was playing at pool missed yet again with the black ball at her mercy. The Aussie would win the game, and keep his male pride intact by a whisker, yet again. Jeab had seen the same tale act out for nearly 30 years, it never ceased to amaze her how these guys were not able to ascertain that the girls controlled who won the pool games. The young girl (who was one of the best bar pool players Jeab had seen) giggled and said

"Oh I so close, you too good player." The young lad gave her ass a rub and sat down signalling for his mate to take the next game.

Pinky thanked Jeab before heading home to move to the next phase of her planning. These quiet moments gave Jeab some more time to ponder her life. She was the epitome of the happy but tough *mamasan* – great banter with the punters, she spoke good English with some nuanced humour and an understanding relationship with her girls. Again, as with so many here it hid a sadness deep within. She was still a striking woman. In her late 50s with smooth dark skin and a wonderfully warm smile, she had adopted a modern shorter haircut when she hit 50 and it definitely suited her. She always dressed tastefully, she had earnt that right. She still had a good figure and she loved how she was now able to dress to merely hint at that rather than be forced to advertise it. She was very glad those days were over.

It was known that Jeab had no children, and no family to speak of, only those who were truly close to her and that she trusted knew the truth. Her darling son, Note, born when Jeab was a young 20-something beginning her life in Bangkok had died tragically in a motorbike accident shortly after his 16th birthday. Jeab had never got over that tragedy, how could anyone? However, she had learnt how to manage the pain. Nearly 20 years after his death and Note was still the first thing Jeab thought of when she woke, every morning, without fail. It was as if every morning she'd wake and have to remind herself that Note was no longer with her. Like so many women she met in Nana, she did what she did for her child, in a desperate attempt to ensure he would have a better life than she did. For his 16 years, Note did. He was doing well at school and was already thinking about going to University in Bangkok, Jeab could see he would have a genuine future. He had the skills and intelligence to excel in everything he did and she was so proud of him. Note was mature beyond his years, and he was aware of the sacrifices his mother made for him in life. He was equally proud of her and showed no shame in letting people know that his mother was a waitress in a bar.

For years after Note's death Jeab felt completely empty inside, she whittled away her savings – they were for Note's future, not hers. However, she had slowly found a coping strategy and a way to put on a mask of normality and had slowly begun to rebuild her life. She had now been running this bar for 10 years and the Japanese owner had complete faith and trust in her. He saw in Jeab a business woman of some ability and was happy enough to give her full control. She managed the budgets, and the repairs and renewals that were needed. She did the books, dealt with all the complicated police negotiations that came from running such an establishment and she turned an excellent profit. She was reasonably well rewarded for her efforts but she was beginning to tire of the daily grind and on days like this she would allow herself to dream of a quieter and more sedate pace of life.

Susie Hoare woke up in the cheap hotel room and let out a sigh. She wondered if you could get early onset Alzheimer's in your late 30s, then she considered that the fact she was even considering the prospect proved that she didn't have it. She was able to rationalise about the joke that her life had become. She knew she was malleable with the truth, the odd white lie here and there, born out of desperation to have her life mean something, to be a success. She had told Tong she would be on a business trip for a couple of days. Far from being impressed he just looked mildly happy but basically disinterested. She had been so full of hope when she had married Tong and their first trip back to the UK together had been a resounding success. She felt like the centre of attention. She showed off about her exotic life in Thailand, with her fascinating husband a real Thai person who spoke this strange language in which Susie claimed fluency. The beauty of this lie was that her British friends had no way of knowing if it were true. She appeared to speak to her husband in Thai and they were impressed.

The truth was that despite her efforts to learn the language she spoke very limited, pigeon Thai of the type spoken by so many foreigners. Her husband could understand quite a bit of what she said only because he had become familiar with her appalling attempts at pronunciation and the depressing fact that their conversations were so limited anyway. In the real world Susie found even ordering simple dishes in a restaurant difficult, such that a baffled waitress would inevitably look to Tong for a translation.

Susie's mother was excited too, for the first time Susie had actually noticed her mother proud of her.

She longed for some grandchildren and she had spoken to Susie about how she would move out to Thailand when the first baby was born to see her through the first months.

"Mum! I'm not even pregnant yet!" Susie would shout back with a big grin on her face. She had begun to try and get pregnant as soon as they had got married. After some months it was clear that something wasn't right. Susie was sure that one of them had a fertility issue but Tong wasn't interested in discussing it and now it had been years, Susie wasn't sure how many, since they had last had sex. Children were now out of the equation and this had become a big unspoken when she phoned her mother.

Susie looked in the mirror and noticed the bags under her eyes, and she began to sob. She usually felt a bit better after letting the emotions flow and she soon began to weep deep tears as she sat and pondered what she would do with this day. Eventually she wiped her eyes and actually shouted out loud to herself "pull yourself together Susie, you've still got it."

She figured she could still be attractive to Tong with a little effort. She could rekindle their love, it wouldn't take much. She could put on a nice dress, go home and surprise him and whisk him away to one of the top hotels in town for a few romantic nights; champagne and bubble baths. They could get the romance back and perhaps could even begin to try again for a baby. It's never too late.

She sat daydreaming of finally being able to tell her mother she was pregnant; she could rebuild her relationship with her mother too, and maybe finally amount to something.

She took a long shower and felt so much more alive and then got straight online and booked 3 nights at the Peninsula Hotel by the river. They could stay more if they wanted, forget the cost, this was an investment in their future. She applied her makeup and instantly felt that she looked younger and more attractive, she smiled at herself a big toothy grin. She quickly packed her bags and grabbed a taxi to head back to the apartment she had bought and shared with Tong. For the first time in years she felt a positivity, she had an upbeat look on life and it had just taken a few tears and a little bit of clarity of thought. As she jumped out of the cab back at the Condo down the Phetburi Road end of Asok road she felt very much in a 'what might be' mindset. She got out of the lift and walked towards the apartment door with a nervous anticipation. She felt like a teenager again, about to ask a boy she liked to go on a date. She paused outside her apartment door to compose herself, and neatly apply her red lipstick. What she saw when she opened the door would indeed change her life, forever.

NINETEEN

Pinky decided now was the time to move things along with Marshall. She felt that everything had been going so well in her manipulating conversations with him. She now felt sure that Marshall was going to propose the very idea that she was carefully trying to move towards. He himself seemed to be scaling things up. Pinky had adeptly engineered a situation where it was clear that Marshall saw Pinky as a loyal friend. Pinky has slipped it into conversations that Ting was more of a casual acquaintance than a friend and that she only knew Tang from his frequent visits to Bangkok. She revealed this with a degree of subtlety that enabled Marshall to think he was working things out slowly. It was important to Pinky that she didn't reveal any genuine details of where Ting was, always being vague and eventually choosing Khon Kaen as the place Ting was from, 'somewhere near Khon Kaen', was usually enough to satisfy Scott

Marshall.

"Ting ready to meet with you *Khun* Scott, but I not tell her anything about your plan." Pinky, told Marshall in her typically off-hand way.

"Pinky you little beauty! I can't thank you enough. When is she coming?"

"No, she think it good you meet somewhere else, somewhere nearer her home. She know a nice place near Khon Kaen, very romantic."

Hearing this sent shivers down Scott's spine, how typically thoughtful of Ting, sweet Ting, wanting to meet somewhere special. He even wondered if Ting had the same plans as him. Soon, it was all arranged. Pinky and Marshall would travel to Khon Kaen and meet up with Ting at the Khon Kaen Spa Resort, where they would have a lovely few days and Scott and Ting would plan their future together.

It had taken Pinky some time to persuade Ting to meet up again with the American, she was still concerned about the stolen money and their night in Bangkok, but she trusted her friend knew what she was doing. Everything was falling beautifully into place.

Nam was upset when Ting told her she was leaving. Although Ting had assured her it was only for a few nights, Nam didn't know what to believe. She had been so happy to hear Ting was considering moving back to Nong Khai to be with her family, and for her to be leaving so soon made Nam wonder if she had already changed her mind. Ting didn't want to involve her mother with the sordid truth, it would only worry her, and Ting herself didn't know how this was going to play out. She packed a few possessions, some make up and her nicest clothes, and got Tang to drive her to the bus station in Nong Khai. She had explained to Tang and her mother that Pinky had invited her to spend a couple of days in Khon Kaen with friends. She gave them the flimsiest of details but assured them both that she would be back in a matter of days. Tang knew her sister was in good hands, Pinky was a sensible woman and he had felt confident that despite his sister's odd behaviour she would indeed return in a couple of days.

The Khon Kaen Spa Resort had opened two years earlier, evidence of the growing affluence of Khon Kaen. Set on the edge of town surrounded by rural plots there was a pleasant calm and quiet atmosphere. It had gained a good reputation with Khon Kaen's elite, who would visit for drinks in the bar overlooking the fields or for a Sunday brunch. It was a great place for the family and every Saturday they put on a traditional *Isaan* dancing festival with a fantastic buffet to match.

Pinky had arranged for the hotel to send a car to pick up Ting from the bus station, Marshall had insisted that Ting be treated with the class and style she deserved. It had made Ting feel very important to see her name up on a sign at the station, a little bit like you see in an airport, though she also felt a bit embarrassed. She was convinced that people were watching her and judging her, that she was trying to pretend to be something she wasn't. She was happy when Pinky explained she would arrive at the hotel before them as it gave her a few hours to relax and compose herself. The room was beautiful and there were pleasant views out over the fields. This surprised her as she had found Khon Kaen to be a slightly dusty and non-descript industrial town on the drive to the resort. She had a long shower and enjoyed putting on the hotel's soft cotton robe as she got ready for the meeting with Marshall. Pinky texted her to say they were on the way to the hotel and that she should meet them in the lobby café. Ting dressed and slowly wandered along the winding path to the café, she ordered herself an iced coffee and waited with trepidation.

Despite Alf Hayes moderate successes in the drug business of Nana, he was still a relatively small time player in the game, even if he was acutely unaware of this fact himself. He sold in modest quantities to a large number of small time petty dealers, some who were users and indeed borderline addicts themselves. For the likes of Valeriy Dublachenko this was classic amateur stuff. Dublachenko always kept himself more than an arm's length away from the street, so to speak. There were three trusted middlemen who did the bulk of the selling work in his operation; a hotel manager, a record producer, and the third a full time drug dealer. However, they still had no contact at all with Valeriy and knew little about him, Valeriy only dealt with three senior employees of his operation in whom he had total trust.

To the casual observer Valeriy Dublachenko was simply a successful Russian property developer, exporter, and investor. Indeed he did own a string of condominiums in Bangkok and Pattaya and he was currently developing a second hotel, a small 20 room resort on the Eastern Seaboard between Pattaya and Rayong. The profits of his illegal business empire had to go somewhere and this was the best way Valeriy knew to launder money. The hotel would have a bar, restaurant, offer day trips, spa treatments, bus services into town – a vast array of opportunities to put dirty cash through the books which would come out pristine at the other end.

Valeriy was exceedingly careful to do many things strictly above board. The money that he initially put into condo purchases in Bangkok all looked clean with a paper trail that led back to the sale of his property in Moscow some years back. The new resort would make the laundering of cash so much easier and of course officially it would therefore be making large profits, regardless of occupancy. The reality of course was that few questions would ever be asked. He already owned a mid-range hotel in Pattaya and his was one of the few businesses that paid all taxes honestly and voluntarily. His accounts and auditing were done professionally and he was also extremely generous with the local police and politicians, as well as generously funding some well-respected local charities. In short, Valeriy Dublachenko knew how to run a criminal enterprise in the way that Alf Hayes most definitely did not.

Dublachenko did however find Alf's company rather enjoyable,at times. It amused him to be in the company of such a loose tongued idiot. They had only met twice previously when Hayes began to speak of his criminal brilliance.

"Hey, Val isn't it?" Hayes spoke with a confident air.

"Valeriy." The Russian replied.

Hayes was oblivious to the fact that Valeriy did not appreciate being called Val. Hayes grilled him about what he did in Bangkok, and then feigned fascination with what he considered the dull world of property development.

"I expect you're wondering what I do here, eh Val?"

Dublachenko simply smirked. Hayes looked from one side to the other, as if he was about to reveal some big deep dark secret.

"Well ask around the streets mate, you'll hear. What doesn't Big Alf Hayes do? I fucking run this town pal!"

Dublachenko was both curious and amused. "You!?"

"I can't say too much of course my Russian friend. But you name it I can sort it out for you. Know what I mean?"

"No."

The Russian continued in one word answers.

"Haha the world of property development has you too sheltered mate! I'm talking sex, drugs and rock and roll! What you want Alf Hayes can get. You want drugs? You want a youngster? Leave it to me."

Dublachenko flashed Hayes an angry and offended look.

"I don't mean you as in you! Fuck no mate. I mean other people. Stick to houses mate, you wouldn't believe the sort of people I deal with. Different world out there pal." Hayes waved his arms around to emphasise his point.

They met and chatted every so often, the conversations always followed a similar tone. Hayes would talk more and more, revealing every secret he had. Dublachenko would just listen, nod and add very little to any conversation. After all, what could a mere property developer add to a conversation about the criminal underworld in which Alf Hayes evidently thought he knew so much.

The Russian knew it would do him no harm to be kept informed as to what the likes of Hayes were up to. It helped him find plenty of information about what was going down on the street, and despite their different approaches and style they were after all in the same business, albeit at differing ends of the scale. It wasn't unheard of for small time players to start taking too big a slice of the pie and it would be useful for Valeriy to be aware should there be any danger of that happening.

TWENTY

Aside from the huge increase in sexual appetite, Tong also found that getting high like this made him talk, a lot. He talked and talked openly about his life, his family, his marriage, his sexuality. His Australian friend just sat and listened intently, smoking to get himself deeper into a euphoric yet calm state. Of course every so often this would be interrupted by another sexual episode but there was more talking than sex over the course of the night.

He talked about his family back in Nong Khai and how he now gave more and more thought to being back there. He had grown to dislike Bangkok after his initial excitement at moving there. He felt trapped. Trapped in a marriage to Susie and financially trapped – he wasn't working and he lived in an apartment that Susie had bought, albeit in Tong's name. Tim was curious. Was Tong in love with Susie? Did he really like women as well as men? Tim found this hard to imagine from his previous rendezvous with Tong.

Tong couldn't honestly answer yes to either question. The bisexual label seemed an easy option for him when he wasn't quite confident enough either with himself or others to honestly say he was gay and going both ways seemed to be so convenient. Then he met Susie and of course he was flattered by the interest and impressed by her apparent wealth and her hi-so contacts. If he was honest it also just simply seemed cool, exciting, and different to be with a *farang* women. He'd known plenty of Thai girls who had married foreigners over the years but there weren't so many Thai men marrying *farang* women and he certainly didn't know any. This novelty factor kept him going for a while. Holidaying with Susie in nice hotels and spending time with her *farang* friends (who seemed to be remarkably few in reality). Then they were buying a condo and choosing amazing furnishings. It was like living a dream for Tong. The dream soon faded though, and the reality began to creep in. Before he knew it he was stuck in a loveless marriage with someone he increasingly found he disliked. At times he felt he detested her. Her looks, what little she had, were gone. But that physical shallow aspect was obviously never really an issue for Tong anyway. He disliked her character too. The lies, the delusion, the volatility – he'd had more than enough.

Tim listened intently. Occasionally he would affectionately rub Tong's shoulder. He asked him, matter of fact

"have you ever been in love Tong?"

Tong had been in love, once. It still made him sad thinking back to his best friend from high school, the only person who he had ever truly loved and perhaps the only person who had ever truly loved him. He had never been able to tell Big how he felt. He lived with that pain, that niggling 'what if?' in the back of his mind. Tong had met Big when they were 13, they were in the same school and they quickly became the best of friends. They were almost inseparable, spending all their free time together either at each other's houses or simply hanging out in the small town they lived in. They'd spend time milling around the local shop, buying snacks or generally causing mischief. They had always been very tactile in a best friends type way and it was only when they were about 16 that Tong started to become aware that his true feelings for Big went deeper than traditional friendship. He always wanted to be with Big, he always thought about him, he longed to hug him to feel the warmth of Big's body close to his. Soon after they began to discover beer it seemed that Big had begun to discover girls too, at least he talked about girls a lot. Which ones he liked, which ones had nice bodies. He never dated any of them, and Tong would go along with the laddish conversations. Their weekend routine was repeated endlessly; go out, drink some beer (without their parents knowing) and spend the night in one of their beds, together. Tong was in love and he thought many times about telling Big, but he had no idea what Big thought and he was terrified of losing what they did have. There were so many nights when they would be intertwined together, in bed. Tong wondering if it meant the same to Big. They were never overtly sexual together, but for Tong it was incredibly sensual; a sensuality he had never felt since. There were some nights when he would kiss the back of Big's neck or gently nibble his ear, holding each other's hands tight. Sometimes Tong would elicit what seemed to be a contented moan from Big. In Tong's mind they were a young couple in a loving relationship. He just hadn't felt able to talk to Big about it. But it was obvious. Wasn't it? Surely? The time they spent together, the nights sleeping in the same bed, they had to be more than just friends.

Then it happened. On one night at a party with a group of people from their school, Chompoo came into their lives and destroyed everything, for Tong. Tong would never forget that night when Chompoo came to chat with them both. She was flirting ridiculously with Big and Tong found it increasingly irritating how she flicked her hair and laughed at every joke Big made. Occasionally she would brush his arm with her hand or even more transparently actually squeeze his biceps and comment about how fit he was from playing sport. Tong could still remember that feeling of utter devastation and hopelessness when he saw Big and Chompoo walking away together. The following day an excited Big told Tong everything. He didn't know how to react, he felt his world was falling apart. For some painful months he became a friend to the couple but slowly they began to drift apart and Tong found that the pain of being away from Big was easier than the pain of seeing his true love with Chompoo. The last Tong heard, Big had moved to Chiang Mai. He never asked more. He didn't want to know. It still brought back too many painful memories.

Tong sat quietly and was only brought out of his saddened haze when he realised that Tim was back on the floor with his head between Tong's legs and ready to service him again. He put his head back on the top of the sofa and felt totally calm and relaxed as the door to the apartment opened.

Ting and Pinky had discussed at great length how the meeting with Marshall might go, but of course no amount of preparation could make them entirely sure how things would play out. Pinky saw Ting sitting in the hotel lobby bar and remembered thinking how radiantly beautiful she looked. The youthful skin, that twinkle in her eyes coupled with that clear look of shy apprehension on her face. She felt a momentary rush of guilt, what had she got this innocent sweet girl into? After all, if she was honest it was technically criminal what they were planning to do. There was a slight breeze blowing through the open-air lobby and Ting's hair casually blew in the wind, only adding to her stunning appearance. She looked like a film star and Pinky considered how unjust life was. Ting probably had many of the attributes of those Bangkok hi-so celebrities, and yet her life had been in many ways fixed from birth simply by the pure chance of being born into a family of relatively poor subsistence farmers up in Nong Khai. This was a constant in Pinky's life, this deep feeling of frustration of the way life went for girls like her and Ting and how so many people looked down and formed hard-wired stereotypes about them. Even worse, she mused, the ones who pitied them 'These poor girls have no skills, so have to sell their bodies. It's so sad.'

How ignorant they were. Pinky was every bit as capable as anyone in Thailand, in her opinion. It was just that so much of her life had been dealt from the stack of cards at birth. Of course there were always exceptions to the rules, but they were just that, exceptions. The hard, harsh reality remained. In Thailand, just like everywhere else your life was to a large extent mapped out from birth. It wasn't fair, and Pinky figured this plan with Ting was one way to start pushing back against these immovable forces of fate.

When Scotty Marshall saw Ting he let out an audible yelp, rather like a wounded dog might if someone stepped on its tail. Tears began to well up in his eyes as he ran over to the table where Ting was sat.

"Ting, my Ting. My Love. My one and only."
At that moment Ting and Pinky were relieved there were no other people sat in the bar to witness this embarrassing scene. Pinky subtly motioned to Ting that she should stand up to greet the American. He hugged her hard, uncomfortably hard, as he made a sort of groaning noise. It was hard to distinguish exactly what this noise was. Ting managed to utter the words she had practised with Pinky in the run up to this meeting

"I love you very much. You good man for me."
This brought another audible yelp from Marshall's lips. The awkwardly long hug was then followed by an equally awkwardly long silence which Pinky broke by suggesting they sit down to order a coffee, and chat.

The conversation was, just as one might expect from a couple deep in love.

"Ting you are even more beautiful than I remember."

"You so handsome, think you not so fat now." Ting said with minimal confidence and sincerity.

"Oh I'm so glad you've noticed. I'm on a diet, so I

can look my best for my sweet Ting."

The truth was that Marshall looked just as Ting had remembered, but Pinky had explained that these overweight Americans loved being told that they weren't as overweight as they had been previously.

"I was so worried Ting, I thought you had been kidnapped."

Once Pinky had translated this, Ting again went into a well-rehearsed speech.

"I ok *Khun* Scott. My brother Tang, he good man. He just *kidteung* Ting and want me stay with family." Ting would occasionally slip in the odd Thai word and Pinky would have to translate. Marshall found this wonderfully endearing.

Ting explained that she didn't know Tang had taken Marshall's money from his hotel room and that was not really the sort of thing she would expect Tang to do. Marshall was hooked on every word, and the more Ting insisted she would pay the money back, the more Marshall said he simply would not hear of it. Pinky had explained to him that Tang had only taken the money for the same reason he had come to get Ting in the first place, the family were in dire straits. The rice harvest had been relatively poor and the rubber price had hit rock bottom. She didn't quite go as far as to mention a sick buffalo, but she was getting close. She was worried for her elderly mother. Of course if Nam had heard this tripe she would have laughed, loud, she was far from the epitome of the elderly Thai woman that Marshall was now imagining, but he was in a trance.

Suddenly he got down on one knee, to Ting's utter bemusement, but Pinky had seen enough crappy Hollywood movies to know what was coming next.

From his pocket he took a ring. He had to max out his credit card to purchase the ring at a cost of $2000.

"Ting, when I first saw you so out of place in that bar I knew I had to make you mine. I knew you needed me to guide you through life's journey. Ting My Ting, my sweet sweet Ting, I can't imagine life without you. As my wife."

Pinky was trying to remain composed, but inside she was thinking 'YES! We nailed it!' Ting, who was nicely warming to her role as shy leading lady put both hands to her face in shock and Pinky could see a tear developing in Ting's right eye, she was mightily impressed.

"I love you same *Khun* Scott."

After all the excitement Ting said she had to go to her room to lie down, leaving Pinky chatting with the delirious American.

With Ting now gone, Pinky was able to explain to Marshall that Ting didn't want to discuss the grubby business of money as she was so scared that Scotty would think that she was money oriented like some of those girls she had heard about. Pinky began to introduce her great idea to Marshall, making it abundantly clear that Ting knew nothing of it. Pinky and Marshall were becoming close friends now of course and Pinky presented herself as the official matchmaker who just wanted to see her friends happily married as their undeniable love deserved. This was the line Pinky was using with Marshall and he was taken in by it, unhesitatingly. Pinky's super idea centred around Scotty's thoughts of an American diner but maybe it could be a small hotel as well. Scott began to ponder how unique and amazing it could be. A Thai-American eatery and hotel in the heart of *Isaan*. She quickly had Marshall hooked on the idea. Of course Marshall would need to view suitable plots, put in a negotiating bid, everything would be done properly. She suggested that in two weeks he move to Khon Kaen and start to plan their wedding and their future, and that she would quietly be his agent in the plan to find the dream home and business for the happy couple. Marshall was deeply touched by how much Pinky wanted him and Ting to be happy and he was impressed by Pinky's sharp business brain.

TWENTY-ONE

There were empty bottles on the floor. A coke
bottle, maybe a whisky bottle, and a couple of plastic
water bottles. Susie's eyes initially focused on a small
patch of coke that was pooling on the attractive
wooden floor. The sticky sugary solution seeping its
way into the gaps. She was aware that she was faced
with a scene where a middle aged *farang* guy was going
down on her husband but somehow her brain had
told her to focus on something else. She walked in
and picked up the coke bottle, lightly tutting and
muttering that it might stain the floor. Tong didn't
quite know how to react, he was frozen in a mix of
shock and the hours of getting high. Tim momentarily
looked up at Tong and asked "do I need to stop
mate?" At that Susie marched into the bedroom and
quietly shut the door. Looking back she would
wonder why she didn't slam the door or go into a
wild rage and hurl the empty bottles at her cheating

husband, but she didn't. She quietly closed the door, sat down on her bed and looked vacantly at the white painted wall.

Having got no audible reply and certainly no response from Tong's rigid cock, Tim got back to what he had been doing. Tong sat with a similar vacant stare to his wife and began to contemplate what he should do. Tong wasn't exactly the best when it came to dealing with marital problems and emotions, but who did know what you are meant to do when your wife catches you with a man. It was fully 10 minutes before Tong broke the silence and told Tim that he thought it would be best if he left. The door to the bedroom remained firmly shut as Tong began to process what was going on. He ever so slightly began to laugh. He'd feel guilty about that later but in the moment he let out a quiet, yet audible chuckle. He had spent months, years, wondering if he should just come clean and break up with Susie but he just didn't know how he would ever go about that. Now he didn't have to, job done, over. There was a part of Tong that was relieved that this was all over and now maybe he could actually begin to live the life he wanted, rather than this painfully false existence with Susie.

Tim quietly began to gather his things and get dressed, and he sensitively suggested he'd wash his face in the kitchen sink rather than go into the ensuite bathroom and face the spurned wife. Tim took a few last long drags of the *ya ice* they had been smoking. Tong didn't know what to say.

"Sorry Tim" was all he could muster.

"No worries mate", Tim replied in typically laid back Aussie fashion. As he left he nodded towards the bedroom and whispered "good luck buddy." The front door to the apartment shut with a clunk and the room returned to an eerie silence. Tong returned to sitting motionless on the sofa, still trying to work out quite what he was meant to do. Maybe he would just wait for Susie to do something.

Susie wasn't sure exactly for how long she'd sat still on that bed. She continued to look at the wall in a daze, just above the happy wedding photo that sat on the dresser. She thought how strange life was; just seconds after she stood at that door with positive thoughts running through her mind about working things out with Tong, her whole life had come crashing down around her. She felt ashamed and humiliated. She pondered, why? Why? Why did Tong look so contented sitting with that man? She couldn't remember when she had last seen contentment like that from him. Hell she thought that maybe she had never seen that look of pleasure from Tong at any point when they had had sex. He had always been very clinical. 'That's just Tong' she had just dismissed to herself, many times. Now she realised it wasn't just Tong. It was just her.

She suddenly got up from her trance and removed a big suitcase form the cupboard. She needed more than a couple of night's worth of things. She haphazardly emptied some of her clothes into the suitcase as she began to formulate some sort of plan, such as where the hell she was going to stay. A cheap hotel would do. She considered that most normal people would just phone up a friend. She reached for her phone before realising that there was no-one she could credibly phone. That was the point that actually started the tears to flow. Not that her husband was cheating on her with another man, but that she had no-one in her life to support her through it. She broke down and sobbed deep, heavy tears. Eventually she forced herself to put on a brave face and she opened the door to the living room in the hope that she could leave their marital home with some sort of dignity intact.

For the second time that evening she stood outside the door, suitcase in hand and took a deep breath. Oh the irony.

As the door opened, Tong stood up.

"Susie, I'm sorry. I don't know……"

"Don't Tong, don't." Susie interrupted him. Then as she walked to the main door to leave the apartment, Tong, baffled for what was appropriate asked "are you going back on your business trip?"

Quietly Susie replied "no", and with that she shut the door and walked down the corridor with tears streaming down her face and her shoes squeaking on the newly polished floor.

Marshall had found it rather sweet that Ting didn't feel they should share a room at the hotel, now that they were to be married. She felt it seemed slightly cheap. That's the class of my Ting, thought Marshall. He grinned at her in a way that some might consider a tad patronising. Again, Pinky had done the bulk of the explaining. She told Marshall that Ting was full of guilt about spending a night with him in Bangkok and that her mother would be horrified if she thought her daughter had been with a man outside of wedlock. Pinky explained that Ting wanted to really get to know Marshall more, before the wedding. Of course after that, Pinky joked, they could enjoy a glorious and traditional wedding night. Marshall could barely wait, and yelped again with his excitement. He seemed to have totally blanked out from his memory the small matter of the money that was missing from his hotel room.

With Pinky acting as translator, sometimes in the most creative of ways and sometimes in the most simplistic of ways, Marshall and Ting began to discuss their lives together. Ting seemed very excited about opening Khon Kaen's best hamburger joint, but of course she explained that Scotty shouldn't be investing lots of money in any businesses for him and Ting.

Marshall would animatedly wave away her concerns.

"Ting my sweet. Love has no price. Our union is about love, not money."

Sometimes Pinky didn't really need to translate, the gist was clear. Crystal clear in the tackiest of ways as Marshall made heart shapes with his hands and pumped his chest. They spent two days getting to know each other with Pinky acting as a chaperone and Scotty explaining that his love was growing ever stronger by the day.

Pinky was doing such a good job as negotiator, translator, and business advisor that Scott had begun to ask her if she wanted to be involved in the running of the business. He felt that Pinky was the glue that held his loving relationship with Ting together.

Pinky giggled when Marshall flattered her.

"Maybe in few years *Khun* Scott, but now I working in Bangkok."

Pinky had begun to try and explain some of the

complex property laws in Thailand to Scott, she seemed to be quite the expert and Scott considered how lucky he was to have fallen into this near perfect situation. She had also shrewdly explained to Scott that he had to be totally sure of his love for and trust of Ting. Pinky couldn't be clearer on this point and this was why Scott was quite sure that she genuinely had his best interests at heart.

"I know Ting is a such a nice and honesty girl *Khun* Scott. But I don't want you not love her next year and then be angry with me."

Marshall explained to Pinky that her caring attitude was touching but that not only was he sure of his love for Ting but that it was also clear the business would be a resounding success. 'An American in Khon Kaen', he had even started thinking about a book he might write in the future!

Pinky had said that to get the right site in thriving Khon Kaen they might need to be prepared to act fast, very fast, and that rather than wasting time with Scott starting the painfully laborious process of opening business bank accounts that he should quickly get the funds together and transferred into an account in Pinky's name – a sort of holding account.

"I would be upset *mak* if you lost out on good property because of waste time with banks, *Khun* Scott."

Scott thought this was a very sound idea and he had even suggested that Pinky should take a 0.5% commission for handling the cash and for the hassle it might cause her. Pinky laughed this off again and made it clear to Scott

"I do this for my friends." She did agree that *Khun* Scotty could provide her with free burgers for life when the restaurant opened.

Pinky explained to Scotty that she would get a lawyer friend of hers to write up some papers explaining that she was simply acting as a 'middle man' and would have no claim on the cash that Marshall paid to her. Again, Marshall was amazingly impressed with Pinky's absolute honesty and integrity to do things in the correct way. They had begun to discuss sums. Pinky had thought that $100,000 was more than enough, but Marshall explained he wasn't doing anything on the cheap and that he may as well transfer her double that, as this was the value of his major savings fund. This would also cover the wedding, honeymoon and any general settling in costs he would have. After all, emigrating to Thailand was a major undertaking.

They agreed to meet up in Bangkok in a couple of days to start thrashing out the details. It was the last night in Khon Kaen and Marshall began to get quite emotional. He would soon have to say goodbye to his beloved Ting for maybe 2 or 3 weeks. He hated the thought of this, having just been reunited with her and Ting having lit a fire within him. Tears welled up in his eyes at the airport the next morning when he waved goodbye to Ting and walked through to the departure lounge for his flight back to Bangkok.

TWENTY-TWO

Two weeks passed and as February became March so the unmistakable Bangkok heat returned. The few weeks of cooler weather at the start of the year were but a temporary respite. The locals were relieved as this year had brought an unusual 'cold snap' in which the temperature had actually dipped below 20c for part of two days. Meanwhile, the city's hordes of expats began to start their annual moan about how hot it was, how they had never known it so hot, definitely hotter than the previous year and so on. They never tired of these endless weather conversations, and it wasn't just the British. It was like the Brits had spread their weather-obsessed culture to other *farang* in town. You'd hear French and American expats happily taking part in the same mundane weather conversations.

For Bob Lowe, the sweat levels would soon be up to what he called 'Lowe Max', and he could only hope that he was out of the plasters on both legs before the heat intensified even further in April. The truth was that Bob was making a surprisingly quick recovery, by some remarkable fluke the second knee replacement had helped to fix a minor error that Dr Brown had made on the first. The antibiotic cocktail had worked and Lowe was infection free and able to slowly get about town with the aid of crutches. Lon was readying to move out, and it couldn't come quick enough for her. She had managed to extract small amounts of spending cash from Bob, but this was always going to be more of a favour to Alf Hayes than a big earner. Bob seemed to have got it into his head that he and Lon were a fully-fledged couple, his pain killer addled brain seemed to have forgotten that Lon was very much 'on hire', as a temporary arrangement.

"My dear Lon, do you like living here? Should we move somewhere else?" Lowe mused to his 'beloved' over breakfast.

Lon looked at Lowe, indifferent.

"Up to you, move where you like."

Up. To. You. Three words that epitomised Thailand for Bob Lowe, and just why he loved living there so much. Women in Bangkok were happy to let the men lead. Bob was all for equality of course but he felt things had gone too far in the UK. When Bob tried his luck with a British woman in a pub they just gave him a look with such attitude. 'They think they own the place' Lowe would hollow to his friends. Yes, things had gone too far.

"But Lon, I want you to be happy where we live."

Lon gave a confused look, "Why I care where you live Mr Bob. You live Rayong if you like. I no care."

Bob flashed Lon a patronising smile.

"Lon, Lon, we're a pair now, doubles partners, together. We. Us. The Lowemeister and the Lonster. Legendary!"

Now Lon laughed. Not just a normal laugh. This was a real, out of control hysterical laugh. Lon couldn't remember when she had last laughed like this. Certainly not during her brief employment as Bob Lowe's nurse, maid, and lover! It felt good, that wonderful feeling to just totally lose control and be chuckling deep deep laughs. She knew it was wrong, and she could see the disappointment in Bob's face, but she was totally lost in the moment and unable to do anything about it.

"Me?! You?! Hahaha, *farang ting tong*, why I live with you?!"

Tears of joy were streaming down her face. She had to grab a handful of tissues (luxury soft ones that she had purchased with Bob's money, much to his consternation.)

"Sorry Bob, not laugh more." She spluttered out through the laughs.

Bob felt crushed. In that moment he was completely aware of his feebleness. He was nothing. Even in the eyes of the very hookers he once lauded it over, he was an irrelevance. Tears began to well in his eyes. Later Bob would reflect that he couldn't remember when he last showed that sort of emotion. He tried to brush it off to himself with bravado, that it was a result of all that medication that had rendered him not quite a catch in the eyes of Lon, a mid-range working girl.

The same episode that had crushed Bob had served to give Lon something of a boost. Life wasn't too bad she thought as she left Bob's apartment. She grabbed Bob's wallet from the table, declaring "now for my tip!" She removed the 4000 baht that he had in there and threw the wallet back towards Bob, declaring both "*Chok dee*" and "sorry Bob ka" as she left his squalid hovel.

A few *sois* away Susie Hoare was still struggling to come to terms with her own feelings of devastation. The previous two weeks had made her acutely aware that she had lost everything; her husband (who was quite visibly looking liberated since Susie left) and her condo. The condo was in Tong's name and he had made it clear he was planning to sell the place. Susie was too depressed and demoralised to even discuss the matter with him. She did still have her job teaching English in a Thai School. She had worked there for approaching 5 years as she continued to maintain this façade of her various successful businesses. She had managed to dwindle her life savings to nothing as she attempted to act out some sort of pseudo hi-so life.

She had now found a cheap apartment two floors down from Pinky and Mint and she was desperately trying to put a positive spin on her predicament. Fresh start. Rebuilding. Life starts at 40. She had used every cliché, and she had a glut of self-help books piled by her bedside table as she tried to find a solution to her hopeless life. Three nights earlier she had built up the courage to tell her mother the truth, and while Mrs Hoare had done her best to display some empathy and show that she could be a caring mother, Susie could hear the disappointment in her voice as she uttered

"Oh Susannah."

It sounded like simple pity. Empathy was a step too far for the octogenarian and what Susie really heard was her mother saying

"You've let me down again," confirmation that Susie was just one big disappointment in her life. Susie's younger brother had always been the favourite child and since he'd tragically died from leukaemia in his mid-20s, Susie's mum had practically given up pretending she didn't have a favourite. In one argument they had two years earlier, Mrs Hoare had icily and softly stated "oh how I miss my Alex." The message was loud and clear, leukaemia took the wrong child.

Susie used to think these things over and over, yes it got her upset and often tearful but it also got her angry and this was her way to try and fire herself up into taking action. She longed to rid herself of this feeling of trying to match her mother's expectations, or of caring at all what she said or did to her, but it wasn't easy.

Susie had been going through a similar routine for the last few weeks. Lots of tears and anger, then a nice long shower, put on some make up and head out. A nice restaurant, a good film, something to try and make herself feel happy and more confident. Always alone, she had no real friends here but she told herself she enjoyed the peace and solitude. Good thinking time. Clear her mind, plan this brand new and exciting future. On this particular night she thought she'd get herself dressed up and go for a nice quiet drink. There were a few nice bars on *Soi* 22, that she considered acceptable for a confident *farang* woman to have a couple of cocktails and watch the world go by. She pondered that she might even get some attention from a nice young barman. Why not? Stranger things have happened. She ordered herself a Pina Colada which arrived with two large slices of pineapple protruding from the side of the glass, with a cocktail stick pushed into it holding a small glace cherry, a mini cocktail umbrella and a straw. Susie struggled with all the paraphernalia, as the straw bobbed out and one of the pineapple slices dropped onto the table. She saw a recognisable figure struggling down the *soi* on crutches.

Bob Lowe couldn't walk well enough to make his way to Nana or *Soi* Cowboy, and Bob didn't waste money on taxis, so he was actually quite pleased to see a familiar face sitting on one of the tables outside 'Paradise'.

"Hello Susie! You're looking well". She wasn't, but Bob always tried to sound courteous.

"Thanks Bob, what happened to you, are you ok?" Susie asked, genuinely curious.

Bob updated Susie on his trials and tribulations. Not the truth of course, but the story Bob had decided on. That his recent exploits on the golf course (in reality Bob had twice been to a driving range some years earlier and was so mal-coordinated that the staff had to put him alone on the upstairs row of the range) had resulted in a cruciate ligament problem in both knees.

"Would you believe that?" Bob exclaimed.
Bob went on to explain that he was becoming quite an accomplished golfer and this setback was a dreadful disappointment to him. He had even been considering that he could in future become a pro on

the senior tour, but that had probably gone now. Susie understood little of what Bob was waffling on about, but she was fascinated nonetheless.

TWENTY-THREE

Marshall had a spring in his step for the full two weeks as he began the process of planning his move and new life with Ting in Thailand. He reflected how things always seemed to work out, just when he was at a really low point in his life something would always turn out for him. 'You lucky bastard' he would chuckle to himself. He was under no illusions as to the luck he'd had in life. Some of his friends from his army days had no such luck having been forced into combat through a combination of their lacking in choices, education, and skills. Marshall had chosen the path he took and he had no regrets on that score. Serving his country, he felt, was the most rewarding thing he'd ever done. But now was a new chapter, becoming a dad again in his 50s might be a challenge but he was sure Ting would be a wonderful mother. He had been in constant communication with Ting, almost always via the 'LINE' text messaging app as

Ting was shy to speak on the phone. On occasion Marshall had insisted on calling her to hear her voice, and he was sure her English was improving. He had been reading up on raising bilingual children and what the best approaches were. He would always speak to them in English, and Ting only in Thai. He would of course learn Thai, he felt 6 months would be enough for him to become fluent, so he would always understand Ting and his kids. He would continue to address them in his native tongue though. He had explained all this in great detail to Ting, and she had been very silent, which he knew was just a result of her excitement at having children and starting this new family life. This was Ting, his Ting. Whether she was really excited, happy, or nervous she tended to react in the same way – by getting very quiet and often she tried to change the subject. It was really very sweet. He knew Thais were superstitious and guessed she didn't want to jinx things by talking about them too much. His love for Ting was growing by the day and although Ting never expressed herself in this way he could feel that it was mutual; 'unspoken love' that's what he called it. That was also the working title for his book about their love story. Initially he had considered 'Letters to Ting' but 'Unspoken Love' was so much more powerful. Love is shown by actions, not words. He could tell Ting was as smitten with him as he was with her.

He was in regular communication with Pinky, given that she was so important to him as a liaison to Ting. Ting's English was not great, he was in no denial about that and so Pinky was an invaluable help in explaining things when needed. Of course, Pinky's real job from Marshall's perspective was to persuade the sweet proud Ting to allow Scotty to spoil her, to treat her to the fineries of life, and to invest his life savings in their joint futures. He was beginning to understand things from Ting's perspective a little more. He had read so many tales now of these so-called 'bar-girls' and the ridiculously gullible men who they dated, just for money. Some of the stories he had read were about girls being bought houses and cars and then they'd tell the man to get lost. Marshall knew Ting must have been horrified at the idea that anyone could think she was one of those girls. Her honesty and integrity was just another thing that made Scotty Marshall love her even more. She was unique. She was the one, finally a true soulmate. Scotty didn't want to patronise Ting; she was young and so her fears were understandable, but in his own mind the idea that anyone could think Ting was one of those girls was so ludicrously farfetched.

Pinky had done a great job for Marshall in explaining that in Scotty's culture marriage was an equal bond, 'What's mine is yours'. It was irrelevant which one had more money, just a total coincidence. If Ting had been the one with more money, then that too would be for both of them. Scotty welled up when Pinky explained that Ting was adamant that her entire life savings of 31,000 baht should be put into the business 100%. Scotty went silent on the phone and then Pinky could hear him sobbing. It was an astonishing gesture and one that confirmed that they were indeed 'one'. Ting even sent Scotty a text

"What mine is you. I tell bank give my money for *Pee* Pinky."

How lucky he was indeed. Scotty had to spend plenty of time on the phone to his banks and investment companies in the US, and had to sign plenty of forms. The cost of the Fed-Ex express services were mounting. He took a bit of a hit as he was cashing in a number of investments early, but he kept telling himself it was about the big picture. This was an investment in his future, both personally and financially. He had never felt so bullish. In readiness of the purchase of a suitable property for their American Diner, Scotty had transferred $208,000 into Pinky's bank account and Ting had done the same with her 31,000 baht. Scotty had signed the paperwork that said that the money was not for Pinky but that she was holding it to act as an agent to purchase a property for Ting. Pinky had someone explain some of the key phrases to Scotty which almost upset him.

"This is not necessary Pinky. Trust Pinky. Trust. You. Me. Ting." He would point to his head and then to Pinky's head to confirm that there was some kind of strong mental connection between them. All was in place though and Scotty could barely contain his excitement. He kept telling himself to keep calm, but how could he. His life had changed in a flash. On Saturday he would travel with Pinky to Khon Kaen where she would take him to Ting's family home, where he would stay. Yes, he would stay with Ting and her family. What a wonderful opportunity for him to get to know the whole family and to meet the woman who brought the amazing Ting into the world and ultimately into *his* world. He was sure he would immediately feel a strong familial tie to his new, soon to be mother-in-law. Pinky had explained to Scotty that they could stay living in the family home until they found a suitable location for 'Ting's Place', the newest eatery in town.

On Friday night Marshall went for a stroll down to the bar where he had first met Bob Lowe and Alf Hayes, and true to form there sat Lowe, with both legs in plaster and sitting with a middle aged and slightly frumpy European woman.

"Hello there, Bob isn't it?" said Marshall cheerily.

"Yes that's me, err sorry have we met?" Lowe was genuinely perplexed.

Even when Marshall explained how, when and where they met Lowe was none the wiser, but he explained that he had just had surgery and of course he remembered. Somehow Marshall felt a smug superiority. There was Lowe, down on his luck, never having met a genuine Thai beauty and here he was about to start a new life with the delectable Ting. He filled Bob and Susie in on the full story.

"Be careful mate, just don't hand over much money to her until you're sure." Bob tried to tone down his warning so as not to sound too cynical.

"You old cynic Bob, Ting's far too proud and genuine to take my money. I have transferred my investment, and make no mistake this is a shrewd business investment, to a dear mutual friend to act as an agent and advisor so to speak" informed a confident Marshall.

Susie could not believe what she was hearing.

"YOU HAVE DONE WHAT?! That money is gone mate." She squealed.

"Gone, never to be seen by you again."

Scotty chuckled in a patronising way. These poor sods he thought. At that very moment his phone buzzed with a text from Pinky.

"Scott, I have to go early now to Khon Kaen. No problem. You go tomorrow. Ting meet you at airport with me."

He momentarily froze. A reaction spotted by both Susie and Bob.

"Trouble in paradise mate?" Susie sneered and Bob gave her a look as if to say, 'Susie, be nice.'

Scott laughed it off. He was sure it was nothing, and again he felt ashamed to have even a scintilla of doubt. These bloody cynical loser Brits had messed with his mind. He shared one quick beer with them, they were pleasant enough and Scotty did pity them with their cynical attitude. They'd both been in Thailand for years but Scotty imagined in his short few weeks he had already experienced more of the real Thailand. He returned to his hotel early, he wanted a good night's sleep. Tomorrow would be a big day.

My Darling Tingle,

It's only a matter of weeks since we first met, but my whole life has changed in that short time. Both our lives have. I am sitting her in this hotel in Bangkok with apprehension and excitement. Of course I am a bit apprehensive, even though I know I have no reason to be. The mind can be an illogical beast Ting, and things have never gone quite this perfectly for me in life. I don't expect to be living out a dream life, and yet here it is, I am! It's like I am in a movie, the perfect love story, the coming together of two cultures. I have to pinch myself to be sure that this is really happening. I've met the woman of my dreams and I am the man of her dreams. What are the odds?! She has a radiant beauty and sweet innocence but a sharp brain, oh yes a sharp brain. Tomorrow I leave my old life behind. The old

Scotty Marshall is no more. I keep imagining that moment when I see you at Khon Kaen airport, there to greet me with a beautiful smile on your face. I feel like I will be returning home, to a home I've never even been to. You will be an amazing mother to our children Ting. We better get started on that straight away! I have so many ideas for our American Diner, I can't wait to tell you. Our American Diner! I am saying those words out loud Ting! Tomorrow I will meet your mother. It will be an awesome moment, and I am so excited, honoured to be meeting her. I will have the utmost respect for her and I am sure she will quickly see how strong our bond is Ting. I love your mother already Ting, look who she has brought into this world. What an amazing woman. Ting my sweet, you are my one and only, my forever, my Ting.

Your loving fiancé,

Scotty Marshall III.

In a small farm and homestead just outside Nong Khai, Ting sat down with her mother for an evening meal. Nong Khai was 170km north of Khon Kaen, far enough away from where Scott Marshall was soon to be flying in, ready to start a new life. Ting had bought some grilled chicken and *somtam* from a small restaurant in the village. She wanted to give Nam a break from cooking and also invited Tang and his family to join. Nam was so happy, she just needed Tong back and then the whole family would be together again. They tucked into the succulent grilled chicken, it had always been a family favourite. Ting and Tang laughed as Nam accepted a bottle of Leo beer. It was rare for Nam to drink alcohol, but she felt like she had something to celebrate.

TWENTY-FOUR

Jeab had given plenty of thought to Pinky's offer. The easy option, she knew, was to stay in Bangkok managing this bar. She looked at her life, it hadn't been easy but she had always manged to make things work. She had come to the conclusion, perhaps inevitably, that the easy option was never going to be the right one for her.

She woke that morning and as always had looked over at the photograph of Note, that was on her bedside table. It had been taken just a month before his motorbike accident. He had a big radiant smile and a glint in his eye, Jeab was no impartial judge but by anyone's standards Note was the very epitome of beauty. He attracted the interests of both boys and girls alike, he had that infectious personality that people just wanted to be around. For a teenager, Note was relatively serious, he had real depths and a maturity that belied his years, but his smile, *that* smile.

It could light a room. Not in a clichéd way in a real and genuine way, when Note was anywhere people were happier. No-one had a bad word to say about him, an extraordinary human being whose time was too short. Jeab began to cry, she didn't often break down in tears these days but sometimes it just came and she would sob uncontrollably. Nearly 20 years after Note's death and still some days she would sob like she had just heard the news. Sometimes she recalled a conversation she had overheard between Note and one of his best friends. The friend had been moaning about his mother not letting him do the things he wanted to do, probably not staying out late or something. He asked Note how things were with his mother. Note paused, and then said "she's like an angel looking down on me, only she's real." Tears welled up in Jeab's eyes both then and now, 20 plus years later.

After Note's death she had spent plenty of time speaking to people, with friends, and at the temple. She took great comfort in many of the words they said, and it did help. She looked so fondly at the times she spent with Note and she was grateful for the 16 amazing years in which he had blessed her life. But no-one could really prepare her for how it felt to lose a child. The emptiness, and the simple fact of missing him, every day, many times every day. She couldn't rationalise that in any way, and nothing would help. Sometimes she just wanted to hug him, to hear some of his zany stories, to cook his favourite meals, to share any aspects of her life and just to spend time with the most incredible person she had ever met.

Jeab quickly composed herself. This, was one skill she had learnt; to put her mask on and to look like a normal woman, rather than 'that woman who had lost her son'. She had agreed to continue to work in the bar and help *Khun* Yasuo to find a replacement, though she had given him a clear deadline. He was grateful for all her loyalty over the years and she had helped him to hand pick the right person to take over. *Khun* Toey had worked in the bar since the day Jeab became the manager, and although she looked a lot younger than her 41 years she rarely picked up a customer anymore. She was stuck in something of a rut in Bangkok, the money earning was drying up and she had wondered whether it was time to head back to Korat and spend more time with her parents and her children. Unlike many of the girls, Toey had never really had an ambition or desire to marry an expat bar customer. Bar-girl work had always been a means to an end. She had done well from the work, she had saved quite hard and managed to avoid the excesses of the scene. She hadn't fallen into the drugs and alcohol trap that befell so many of the boys and girls who filled the Bangkok sex worker vacancies. Toey was a remarkably level-headed woman, Jeab had lots of respect for her and so she had no qualms at all in offering her the role of *mamasan* and had agreed to mentor her in the job. In reality Jeab had been training Toey for this job for years and she knew the transition would be seamless. Toey knew everything there was to know about managing the bar, she had been right there by Jeab's side all this time.

Today would officially be Jeab's last day in charge but she promised Yasuo that she would visit monthly to check the books were in order and that everything was being run with the same slick efficiency. Jeab knew this wasn't going to be necessary but it gave

Khun Yasuo peace of mind and he'd been more than happy to offer to pay for Jeab to have a nice weekend in Bangkok once a month. It would make a pleasant change to be visiting the city and stay in a nice hotel, like a tourist. Yasuo owned a hotel and serviced apartment in the Thong Lo area that predominantly catered for Japanese tourists and expats. He was insistent that Jeab was always welcome to stay, no charge.

Jeab arrived for her final day around 3pm. Toey had opened up, as usual, and there were a couple of girls beginning their day shifts. One middle aged man was tucking into a hamburger with a big bottle of Heineken and the girls took little interest in him. If he wanted company he would ask, he wasn't new to the scene.

"Last day, end of an era" said Toey trying to pull on the emotional heartstrings. Jeab chuckled. She had been surprisingly laid back about the big move. She expected to be more upset, 30 years of working the bars of Nana and over 10 years running this successful establishment. She had enjoyed so many aspects of that time, but she was also sure she would not miss it all that much.

"Will you stay here all night?" asked Toey.

"I will be here until closing, I feel that's the right way to end."

Closing was usually around 4am, there were other bars that would cater for the post 4am slot. On occasions they might close earlier, especially if there was a spell when the police were insisting on observing licensing laws, but that usually only happened when there was a new cop on the beat who wanted to negotiate his fee.

Her apartment had been packed up, there were actually very few possessions she wanted to keep and the following day she would load the pickup truck she had rented and begin her road trip to Nong Khai. She would spend a few days in her hometown of Udon Thani as well as visiting a few sites. There was so much in *Isaan* that she had actually never seen and this was the perfect opportunity. She would be ready to start this new venture with Ting and Pinky by the end of the month.

As the lunchtime trade became the early afternoon and the pace picked up, Thai Airways flight TG304 landed in Khon Kaen and Scotty Marshall took a step into what he hoped would be his magical new life.

In the early afternoon Alf had settled himself in for a few drinks in one of the quieter drinking holes he knew. He had been frustrated lately by his failure to find suitable saps to bring his next shipment in from Burma. Ting's brother had told him he was moving to the North East and Bob Lowe had confirmed he was out of the drug smuggling game. Bob describing his experience of netting 5,000 as "one big hit's enough for me."

Despite his swagger Alf had relatively few genuinely good contacts and after the genius of the knee replacement he was out of ideas. Alf had started to formulate an idea on similar lines but it would be hard to achieve. He had considered finding a pre-op ladyboy. He would send her to Burma where the testicles would be replaced by prosthetics, filled with *ya ice*. He would then fund the real male to female surgery in Bangkok. The issues were endless. He couldn't fit enough product into the testes to make the scam work, and the delicacy of the operation was just too risky he felt. Still he was amused and proud of himself for thinking up another plan of sheer genius.

His recent haul had sold in record time and his customers had reported that the quality was superb, a quicker and yet longer lasting high. Alf had verified this himself and although *ya ice* wasn't his favourite of the sinful pleasures he did find a beautiful smoothness as he smoked and gained an almost instant feeling of calm.

He has also become aware that he had a sudden rush of interest from new business. He had a glut of text messages sent to his LINE account from people who had been given his number and told he had some of the best stuff in town. Alf was always a bit unsure of new business, paranoid about the police being on to him, but he never really knew how to judge whether people were trying to trap him or not. So he just tended to ignore any feelings of being unsure. He told himself that if something really wasn't right he would know.

One of the new customers who contacted him was Mr Nat. Unknown to Hayes, Mr Nat was one of Bangkok's most organised and slick *ya ice* dealers. His day job was that of deputy manager of a branch of Thailand Siam Bank in the centre of town. He was also directly employed by Valeriy Dublachenko. Nat was one of only three people who Dublachenko trusted. The others were known simply as Andrei 1 and Andrei 2. If Valeriy could be considered the company chairman then Nat was his CEO and Andrei 1 probably his CFO with the additional responsibility for expansion and company development. Andrei 2 was not as heavily employed in the business and could probably be considered akin to a consultant in charge of security.

Valeriy was both amused and shocked when Nat told him that the portly Londoner had fallen upon a stash of the best quality drugs that the city had ever known. Nat had a few customers mention this to him, hence his immediate intrigue.

There was a moment when Valeriy had wondered if he'd been fooled by the sweaty Brit, but he had quickly dismissed that and accepted that sometimes even the most ordinary people stumbled blind into the world of serious drugs marketing and distribution. These situations were usually straightforward to deal with and Valeriy Dublachenko had realised this would be no different. His sense of fun had been activated by wondering just how easy it would be to extract all the information he needed from this Hayes character. When Nat had texted to let Valeriy know of Hayes' location and that he had settled in for a session Valeriy decided to pop along for a chat.

Thananat 'Nat' Suparatakorn was something of a misnomer in the world of serious drug money. Most people at his level of the business would not involve themselves with the actual users, but Nat felt it was critical that any good CEO maintain some direct contact with his core customers. So while his major distribution was to sell in bulk to 5 trusted dealers he also maintained direct deals with about 8 carefully selected drug users who encompassed the entire spectrum. He had meticulously identified around 8 categories of user in town and carefully maintained a focus group of sorts, one from each category. He had

3 classes of expat; the low life paupers or 'Nana dwellers'. They tended to float in and out of town due to visa difficulties and often worked 'teaching' English in Thai schools. They tended to have ludicrously inflated views of themselves, despite their salaries rarely rising above 50-60,000baht a month, and for many much much less. These were the sort of people who felt their ability to pick up hookers in Bangkok's bars made them some sort of a playboy character. The middle expat was what he considered the financially stable professional, they tended to be long-term settled, some had families, some ran decent small businesses. For many they had simply settled in Bangkok where their skills and qualifications could allow them a better lifestyle. Jobs in this category ranged hugely. He had even known some doctors. There were still a few teachers, but these tended to be from the International Schools who catered for Thailand's wealthy. The top tier was a very small wedge of his business and he had even wondered if this still merited a category of its' own. These were successful executives; they tended to be more peripatetic workers who would be parachuted into town on 3-year contracts as high level business leaders on huge financial compensation packages.

The local base Nat had split into 5 categories. In many respects this mirrored the system of the expats but with his deeper knowledge of his own country he had some further sub-divisions, such as a split in the upper echelons between new-money and old-money. It was fascinating to Nat, the differences in behaviour and attitude in all these categories.

Nat had first been alerted to the quality of Alf Hayes' product by an expat from the middle category who he only knew as 'Gerald'. He only spent around 5 minutes every few weeks or so with Gerald but he enjoyed their meetings. The system he employed with Gerald was simple and slick. Gerald would text and say something along the lines of "Hey Nat, can you give me a lift today?"

Nat would then pick Gerald up, in his Mercedes S-Class and drive him the 5 minutes (depending on traffic) to the BTS station at Asok. During the journey Gerald would place 7000 baht in the glove compartment and remove his 2g of *ya ice* which Nat would have packaged inconspicuously. Gerald always looked forward to seeing how Nat would package his goodies. Sometimes it would be inside an empty chewing gum package. Occasionally Nat would actually have bought something from 7-11 and slipped the small zip locked bag of *ya ice* into the packaging. On the most recent occasion it had been a cheap USB lead, over packaged of course and Gerald's *ya ice* was neatly slotted into the plastic casing. Gerald asked if the quality was good, "always Gerald." It was the same conversation every time, but on this occasion Gerald added that a friend of his had some amazing quality and from that it didn't take Nat long to establish the origin. It was that fact that brought Valeriy Dublachenko to once again be sitting at a bar with Alf Hayes.

"Hello Val, how's tricks?"

"Valeriy."

"Sorry Valerie" replied Hayes, oblivious to his dreadful pronunciation. They got chatting, Hayes playing the role of the big shot with knowledge of Bangkok's underbelly and Valeriy playing the naïve businessman who was once again having his eyes opened. Valeriy then proceeded to tell Alf that a Russian friend of a friend (whose role would later be played by Andrei 1) had told him that he bought some, Valeriy pretended to be unsure '*ya ice*?' from one of Alf's dealers some weeks earlier.

"I am shocked. Many people in Bangkok they take this drug? It's the same as cocaine?" Hayes chuckled.

"My dear Valerie, I keep telling you, you do not want to know what goes on in this city". Hayes explained the differences between *ya ice* and cocaine but it was clear that his knowledge was limited to merely knowing about the effects and how it was usually taken. It didn't take much for Alf to go into full details about how he smuggled across the border from Burma, where he had the *ya ice* produced. All the while Valeriy was perfecting his array of shocked and stunned faces.

"You are a braver man than me Mr Hayes. I think you are right – I will stick to property developing!" Both men let out hearty laughs. Alf patted Valeriy on the back.

"You're not wrong there mate. What a world we live in, well we both make some cash at least!"
It was then that Andrei 1 walked into the bar. The remarkable coincidence of this was lost on Hayes, and so Valeriy introduced them before announcing this was all too much for him, he was going for a sauna at his gym, dinner, and an early night.

"I am too old for your fast paced life Alf."

Hayes grinned smugly and nodded before buying two beers for himself and his new friend Andrei.

TWENTY-FIVE

My Dear Ting,

I have to be honest, when I got off the plane at Khon Kaen and then couldn't find you in the airport I panicked. I wondered if something had happened to you or if once again your brother had intervened to keep us apart. My panic turned to sheer terror when I couldn't get a phone call through to you. It was only when I was also unsuccessful in phoning Pinky's number that I realised there was a problem with the mobile telephone network. What a nuisance! And what a ridiculous chain of events! I must have given you the wrong flight details (did I get the day wrong?) and on the very same day your mobile network has crashed. Just another chapter in the Scotty and Ting story. Oh how we will laugh at this one day! The extra day will only make it even more magical when I see your sweet smiling face tomorrow. I have checked into a hotel in town, quite close to a lake which is pleasant enough. The internet suggests it is one of the best hotels in town, but it has very much

161

the feel of a 3-star business hotel. Khon Kaen it seems is really lacking in hotel quality. So perhaps this mobile confusion will prove to be rather serendipitous, it has given me another top idea. We should indeed have a small top class boutique hotel attached to our all American diner. This town is ripe for a bit of quality. Anyway Ting my darling, I am exhausted from the dramas of today, so I will sleep well tonight. I will call your first thing in the morning and we will sort this all out. How stupid of me not to get your address as a back up plan!

Love always and forever,

SM III

Bob and Susie had started to hang out together with increasing regularity. Around three nights a week they would now meet up for dinner, or at least a drink. Both had slowly begun to realise they had quite a lot in common. Not least that their lives had hit rock bottom. They laughed a lot about the moronic American who they had chatted with a couple of nights earlier.

"I really didn't believe there were still people like that so easily taken in by these girls" smirked Susie.

"I know Suse, I mean there's enough on the internet to warn people about these sorts of scams and scammers."

They chatted on and speculated that their time in Thailand and knowledge of Thai culture had them sensitively tuned to these dreadful tales of woe, ipso facto it couldn't happen to people like Bob and Susie. Bob had heard just about every tale imaginable and he had Susie mesmerised by the stories he told. As an expat woman quietly married to a local for years, Susie had less direct involvement with these characters. Bob had known men who had mysteriously disappeared never to be seen again. He'd heard of more than one who was murdered by a wife or boyfriend of his wife. The most recent story was his mate Mark who had met a real 'bad un' and despite how obvious this was he kept taking her back. He had been stabbed in his leg, he once got attacked with an empty whisky bottle (cheap Thai whisky to add to the humiliation). Both instances had him in hospital for a few days. He had been attacked by a Thai man who claimed to be the boyfriend of his girlfriend and he had even got a call from a German man who said not only had he been dating this girl for 3 years but they were now engaged. The German had naturally ended things immediately on finding out about Mark. But poor Mark, so low in self-esteem and self-worth he kept on taking her back on the basis that 'love never did run smooth.' She stole money from him, but cried about her dad's gambling debts, so Mark forgave her. The final straw, when Mark finally saw the light was when he decided to sell his condo, wanting to bank his solid profit. His plans hit a snag when the real estate agent established that Mark was no longer the owner of his condo. He had apparently signed it over to his girlfriend some 18 months earlier. It was the final straw but it still took Mark two full weeks to actually move out and break it off with the girl, Pear was her name. Two weeks in which Pear cried, pleaded, cried some more and explained that her father had put her up to it. Finally Mark had grown a pair, got a backbone and had taken legal action against Pear, at quite considerable cost of course.

Susie couldn't quite believe this tale, but Bob had told her that he didn't even need to embellish the story one iota.

"I told him early on Suse, watch out for that Pear, she ain't as sweet as she seems" explained Bob. "But these younger guys they think they know it all."

"What made you realise?" asked Susie with genuine interest.

"I've drunk on these *sois* for years, I've met so many of these girls…and their 'marks', pun intended! I've got a 6th sense for BS my dear Susie."

And so during this conversation on this particular night was born 'Bob Lowe – Private Investigator'.

"And I could be your sexy secretary or assistant" Susie pushed up her breasts as she spoke, and Bob spluttered his beer before descending into a trademark Lowe smoker's cough. Once he composed himself he declared out loud, repeatedly

"Bob Lowe, PI". "It does have a certain ring to it. Step aside Tom Selleck, Lowe's in town!"

Despite Lowe's horror at Susie's 'sexy assistant' comment, he did see the merits of having Susie involved. Not only did she speak a little bit of Thai but he wondered if he could corner the *farang* female market. He knew there were men who for a fee would keep their eye on Thai girls for *farang* men back in Europe or Japan, but he surmised he could tap into the smaller but potentially lucrative *farang* woman market. After all Susie herself had clearly had her problems with her husband. He laughed out loud to himself when he thought that once again he may be teaming up with a 'Hoare'!

"What's so funny Bob?"

"Life Susie, just life."

Andrei 1 didn't need to put on an especially good acting display to outwit Alf Hayes. After a few beers together Alf was convinced he'd found the latest Bangkok sap he needed to bring his next batch of merchandise back across the border from Burma.

Andrei sat surveying the scene. It was comical really, he was obviously totally out of place in this dive, but the half-wit Alf Hayes had neither the ability to think or the deep perceptive skills to realise. Andrei usually wore a perfectly fitted suit that he had made to measure in one of Bangkok's most exclusive tailors. Not one of the regular Nana or Sukhumvit Road ones, they were often very good but Vichai Singh operated down a quiet residential *soi* and his beautifully furnished establishment created a real feeling of exclusivity, as if one was there by invitation only or visiting a close friend. It was almost true, Vichai didn't advertise. He relied purely on word of mouth so he had a complex family tree of customers by virtue of who had recommended them. On this occasion Andrei left his slick suits at home and wore an old pair of faded jeans and a T-Shirt. He told Alf how he had been in Bangkok for 6 months and was loving it. He was planning on finding work maybe as an English teacher or with so many Russians about he wondered if some Thai girls might be keen to learn Russian. Andrei told Alf how good the ice he got from his dealer was.

"Plenty more where that came from" Alf winked at Andrei.

"Can I get some? Today?"

"Not today pal, I'm having a minor delivery and

logistics issue."

Alf let the last sentence hang, and he could see the disappointment on Andrei's face. This was a dream. It was funny how often this happened in Bangkok, he thought to himself. The solution to all your problems could just walk into the next bar.

"Come to think of it mate we might just be able to help each other here. You scratch my back….. so to speak."

"I'm listening" responded Andrei, trying hard to keep any emotions off his face, which wasn't easy. That one line from Hayes had left Andrei now thinking it would be pretty straightforward to get hold of the source of the best *ya ice* in town and to quickly move this fat Brit out of the way.

Alf began to explain his predicament to Andrei. That he himself couldn't smuggle anything across from Myanmar as a man like Alf Hayes would be noticed. The police can't pin any evidence on him, he explained, but imagine if they were aware that he, Alf Hayes, was going back and forth across the border. What Alf needed was someone who could be trusted and who had the coolness and the right attitude to do the job. He told Andrei he would give him 25,000 baht as well as 10g of produce and of course priority ordering in the future.

Andrei tried to show naïve excitement on his face, without overdoing it of course. He got it just right. Hayes felt he was reeling in a prime catch. In his mind Hayes was already planning for a bigger shipment. He was fed up with constantly looking for these deadbeat morons and his ever elaborate schemes of the knee replacement variety. He'd contact his man in Burma and tell him he wanted a bigger order, same quality.

He was confident he could fit out a mini-van with $500,000 worth of merchandise whilst still being able to blend in and not attract too much attention. The beauty of such a high value item, was that tens of thousands of dollars' worth could easily be concealed in a tiny space.

Hayes then began his embarrassingly poor attempt at reverse psychology.

"Listen mate. I'm not sure about this. You should know you'd be taking a risk." Hayes said in ludicrous mock concern.

"I've never been afraid of a risk, but how risky are we talking?"

"Oh well don't get me wrong mate, I've never had an issue and 99% of the time there is no problem, but drugs pal, is drugs." Hayes felt like he was a master, coolly implying that the risk actually was not much of a risk.

Andrei wanted to choke this guy then and there. This pathetic loser gave serious, professional career criminals a bad name. Andrei played the game though and he managed to 'persuade' Hayes to let him be his key man to go to Burma on a 'tour' and bring the goods back. Hayes explained how beautifully simple it was with him having contacts at the border. He could simply drive the mini-van through no questions asked. It didn't take Andrei long to ensure that Hayes would give him all the locational details he required, just so he could feel completely comfortable in completing this mission. Andrei and Alf exchanged numbers before Andrei left. As he walked out he texted Valeriy to simply inform him that things had gone better than could be hoped and all was looking good.

Alf Hayes sat back and rubbed his ample gut that was stretching the fabric of his cheap T-Shirt. He had a satisfied grin on his face. He couldn't believe how well this had gone, he had his next loser lined up to help make him very rich. Life was good.

TWENTY-SIX

Nam was enjoying having her daughter back and she attributed this to the influence of Pinky. Thus Nam felt very positive about the presence of Pinky in Ting's life. Pinky hadn't gone into details with Nam but she'd explained that she had plans to start her own business and that Ting would play an important part in that. She would earn much more money and be able to provide much more in the way of financial support for her mother. Nam was already enjoying the brand new, efficient air con unit that had been installed in the small house. Pinky had assured her she need not worry about the electricity bills as Ting would be able to take care of that. The truth was Nam found it a bit cold with the AC on high power, but she enjoyed the novelty and as the days and nights got hotter it would feel like such a luxurious indulgence.

Ting felt a little bit guilty about scamming the American out of all that money but Pinky reminded her friend how the American had climbed on top of her that first night, assuming that sex with Ting was somehow his American male right. Pinky had not one scintilla of guilt. She had seen so many of these characters over the years, and each one was as much a lowlife as the next. True, Marshall seemed ok on the surface but she knew he would show his true colours just like the rest of them, given the chance.

Pinky had met so many Western men who would quite happily state that equality had gone too far in Britain/USA/Australia (delete as appropriate) and they liked the fact that Thai women were more open to serving a man's needs. It sickened Pinky; they couldn't go back to the 1950s so they came to Thailand instead and desperately tried to recreate it. She was determined to see things change. In the case of Marshall she felt she was helping Ting take control of the situation. Get the blow in early before he had the opportunity to take advantage of Ting and subject her to a life of looking after an old *farang* guy who would inevitably start looking for sex elsewhere once Ting approached her late 20s. She had seen it all before time and time again. They were never different. She had learnt that the different guys basically didn't go around purchasing women from bars.

Ting also felt more relaxed when Pinky explained how things were, and more importantly when she was reminded just how her family would benefit. Her mother had sacrificed so much to bring up her 3 kids, she had worked so hard just to make ends meet. She deserved to be able to finally start to relax and enjoy life to the full in her 50s. Pinky had told Ting that she'd be able to take Nam on holidays, even to Korea.

Nam loved the Korean TV series she had seen and a trip would be such an exciting event for her. Pinky had already met with builders and planners to discuss the construction of the small boutique hotel and spa that would change the lives of Ting and her family.

Scotty Marshall slept relatively well and he woke with excitement, like a young kid on his birthday. He was convinced that today would be the day his new life with Ting would commence. He immediately tried to call Ting, but still couldn't get through. Either her phone network was still down or Ting was asleep and had her phone switched off. He was beginning to get a little more worried than he had the previous day. What if something had happened to Ting and Pinky on the way to the airport to meet him? A car crash? He began to worry himself and wondered what he should do.

He was acutely aware that he had no other contact details for Ting or Pinky, and he was annoyed with himself for such stupidity. He headed down to have breakfast in the hotel. A typical Thai affair, he ordered the 'American Breakfast' which was a fried egg, ham and toast. He chuckled whenever he had seen ABF on a menu. The first time he saw it he had imagined a tall stack of buttery pancakes with crispy bacon and a generous amount of maple syrup poured over the top.

He continued to try and get a call through to either Pinky or Ting, with no luck, and this continued throughout the morning. By early afternoon he was convinced that something awful had happened.

He found the number for the bar in Bangkok

where he had first met Ting and wondered if Jeab, the manager, could help. He was told that she was no longer working there. His luck really was out. The person on the other end of the phone had clearly misunderstood and thought he was referring to some girl called Ting who worked in the bar. Trying to explain was futile.

He realised he now had no choice but to take things further; he went to the nearest police station. He tried to explain to the men at the desk, with little success, and eventually they got the one policeman who spoke good English to come and help. Niki had studied English at Ramkamhaeng University in Bangkok before returning to Khon Kaen to become a policeman. His English was very solid which could actually be attributed more to his love of Hollywood movies and US TV series than his university degree.

"Yes, how can I help you?" he asked Marshall.

"I'm here to report two missing people. I was supposed to meet them yesterday, at the airport. I think they may have been in an accident, or kidnapped. My dear fiancé and our close friend."

"Ok, could you give me their names?" Niki was immediately intrigued, it's not every day this sort of person walked in with such a story.

"Ting and Pinky"

"Full names please." Niki asked impatiently.
Marshall looked blankly back at the police sergeant. He had no idea of either of their full names. He had no address. No date of birth. He had almost nothing. It didn't take Niki long to assess the situation once he'd ask Marshall a few more pertinent questions. Marshall had explained about the business deal, and eventually Niki had explained that it sounded a little

bit like a fraud case. Marshall became incensed. This was remarkably similar to his experience in Bangkok when his precious Ting had been kidnapped by her brother.

"This is NOT fraud!" he shouted back at Niki, thumping his hand on the desk for effect. He explained that he had knowingly and happily, lovingly given the money to a 3rd party, as his sweet Ting was too proud to take all that money. Even as Marshall uttered these words he still couldn't actually hear just how ridiculous he sounded.

Niki nodded and listened and promised he would contact local hospitals and spread the word out about the 'missing' women. Marshall left the police station a wreck. Emotional and worried he headed to the nearest pub where he ordered a cold beer and began to write another of his letters to Ting.

My darling Ting,

So, here we go again. For the second time in our young relationship I am frantically worried about where you are. At least this time I have the knowledge that it will probably all be ok, just as it was the last time. I am sure there will be a logical explanation to it all. I know we will laugh at this with our children one day. Just in case though, I went to the police today. Another frustrating experience I'm afraid. I know there are lots of tales of foreign guys being scammed by Thai women but I am still incensed he would think such a thing of my sweet Ting and our dear dear friend Pinky. But then I suppose he hasn't met either of you. He doesn't know.

To keep my mind clear I will go around Khon Kaen today. Maybe I can find a real estate agent and start looking for suitable locations or just simply find an empty shop front that could become 'Ting's Diner'. There is so much to do that I may as well get started on ideas and plans. It is so true my beautiful Ting that absence makes the heart grow fonder, I am missing you so much today. I can't wait to see you again. Hopefully that will be tomorrow. I have made a list of all the things to do prior to our wedding. So much to do! Where should we go for our honeymoon?

With total love,

Scotty Marshall III

Pinky had found the perfect plot of land right on the river, quite far from Nong Khai city, in fact it was nearer to the border with Loei province. It was a truly beautiful plot, fitting every requirement. It was important to Pinky that any plot she purchased would not result in driving a local off their land, and again she was fortunate that this site ticked the boxes. The man who had inherited the plot of land from his parents lived in Bangkok with his Bangkokian wife and had no intention of returning to live in the North. Pinky immediately had a vision and began to draw some simple sketches. The location of the main building with attached restaurant would be close to the river so that guests could sit on the outside deck and have a romantic drink overlooking the water. The upstairs of this reception building would house Ting, Pinky and family. The large plot of land would have ample space for initially building 12 exclusive bungalows, half with river views for which they could charge a premium. A large spa would be constructed, with a swimming pool, which would be essential for the oppressive heat of the summer months.

There was also plenty of additional space for expansion and an area where they would grow vegetables and keep some chickens which she thought would go down very well with the customers. They could run day trips and, river cruises; she had so many great plans. She found it hard not to get carried away with excitement. The years she had spent working the bars of Bangkok had enabled her to see a lot of hotels around the country, at all levels of the quality scale. At least once or twice a year she would have a customer who would take her away for a week or so. She had seen it all, 5-star luxury, large beach resorts, cheap bungalows and the modern 'boutique' hotels. It was as if she had been doing years and years of market research prior to opening her own business – thorough by anyone's standards.

She took Ting on a little road trip to view the plot. Ting was blown away, she had no idea Pinky had all these ideas and done this level of planning. She unfurled the architects plans on the bonnet of the car and talked Ting through all the little details. This was really happening. She explained to Ting that a price had been agreed with the seller. A good price she explained, as he was quite keen on a quick cash sale. In fact, Pinky explained, once we sign the documents work can start on the plot within a matter of days. We could be open in 6-9 months she informed Ting. Pinky assured Ting there would be some money left over and she should speak to her mother about whether she wanted her own house rebuilt or if she wanted to move to 'Mekong View Resort and Spa'.

Jeab would arrive shortly to act as project manager for the construction. There was no better person for the job, a shrewd businesswoman if ever there was. She was a tough negotiator too and would deal with any issues with the builders with the minimum of fuss. Pinky and Jeab would move into the existing house on the plot, which would be the final piece to be removed and re-built. It was all planned. Pinky and Ting had an emotional embrace. No words were spoken as they looked out over the river. None were needed.

Back in Khon Kaen Scotty Marshall hadn't slept a wink. He already looked slightly dishevelled with his unshaven face and he went back to the police station and demanded to see *Khun* Niki. Niki was out he was told. So Marshall sat and waited. For three hours he sat in the grubby police station waiting room. When Niki finally returned he looked a bit surprised to see Marshall waiting. Usually these fools worked out what was going on and sheepishly disappeared, embarrassed and humiliated. Not this one.

"Mr Marshall, I have been doing some investigating for you."

"Oh good lord, something's wrong isn't it? Ting! Ting!" His voice could be heard throughout the station. "Well, no news, but there have been no accidents involving 2 women as you describe" explained Niki.

"Well that is a relief. Super. So what's the next step in your investigation? This could be a kidnapping" Marshall mused.

"There is no next step. No investigation, no crime. I'm sorry this is not a police matter." Niki explained.

"NO CRIME!? THEN WHERE IS MY TING!?"

Marshall was beginning to well up and tears began to run down his cheek.

Niki remained calm.

"Mr Marshall, have you considered the possibility that this Ting and her friend are simply relaxing in Bangkok or at the beach spending some of the money you gave them?"

Marshall was furious and stormed out of the police station vowing to sue the Khon Kaen police for negligence if anything happened to his Ting. He walked down one of Khon Kaen's busiest streets, past a newspaper and magazine stall. And there he saw Ting's photo on the front of a Thai magazine. At least it was someone who resembled Ting, in his mind. It was actually a Thai-Swedish actress with an article about the latest in her on-off relationship with one of Thailand's top badminton players. He bought a few copies of the magazine, tearing out all the photos of *Khun* Gift and put them in his wallet.

He looked at the pictures.

"Ting, my darling Ting, I will find you."

He proceeded to wander aimlessly around Khon Kaen city centre showing the magazine pictures of a well-known Thai actress and asking people if they had seen her. Many had, in recent films at the local cinema. Some people looked around for a camera assuming this was some kind of prank that would be uploaded to youtube. After a few days of this *Khun* Niki would have to get involved again when people began to complain to the police of a mentally unstable *farang* man bothering Khon Kaen's good folk.

TWENTY-SEVEN

Alf was deliriously happy to have Andrei lined up
to bring in a fresh delivery. He realised it was extreme
luck to have stumbled across him so soon after Bob
and the double knee transplant episode. He had made
a number of successful smallish trades now. This, he
felt, separated him from the small time dealers who
tried to bite off more than they could chew. Alf had
been testing his delivery methods with relatively
modest, yet increasing quantities. He had not
encountered any problems at all. It was simple. He
had clearly chosen the right border crossing,
developed some very nice methods and by chance
had met some accommodating people as well. Those
that get caught, simply don't have the style and
finesse that Alf felt he had. Now was the time to up
the ante and start making some serious life-changing
cash. The Andrei's of this world were not going to
keep wandering into his favourite drinking holes. So

he decided, scale up the order and then he could just wait patiently until another opportunity arose. If indeed he needed another opportunity at all.

He texted his contact in Burma and explained that he wanted a much bigger order and he wanted it as fast as they could produce. They needed a large amount upfront to buy additional equipment and raw materials, but that was not a problem for Alf Hayes. He had the profits from the previous deal and, after all, one has to speculate to accumulate as he kept hearing. Alf Hayes was happy, and when Hayes was happy he liked to have a bit of 'fun' in a particular Alf Hayes way.

He went down to Nana, into one of his favourite bars and asked for *Khun* Jeab. He was told she had left, moved on. He asked for Ting, and he was met with the same response.

"She's what? Oh no she's fucking not!"

"She gone. Same Jeab" was the simple response.

Hayes was livid. "That little whore owes me big time" he muttered. He saw a shy looking young girl in the corner. Hayes hadn't seen her before.

"What's that?" he asked.

"That Ploy" Toey replied.

"I didn't ask her fucking name love. How old is she?"

"18, new girl."

Toey had never liked Alf Hayes and she figured now she was in charge she might start to be a bit tougher with him. Poor Jeab had owed him some favours, historically, and such was her nature she managed to see a good side, even to Alf Hayes.

"I'll take her. Bring her over."

Hayes got out his wallet and took out the usual bar

fine, plus a bit extra. He was in a generous mood. Young Ploy didn't look too happy when she was summoned over. Perfect, thoughts Hayes. He hailed a cab and told the driver to take him to *Soi* 22, Hayes' back up cheap apartment.

Alf and Ploy had a very cordial, almost pleasant chat in the taxi, which put Ploy more at ease. She had heard of Alf Hayes and didn't much like the idea of spending time with him, but she also knew he had a reputation for being a generous payer. She was sure a lot of the stories must be exaggerations, no one could be quite that bad. He even seemed quite likeable she thought. She saw he gave the taxi driver a 20-baht tip, a good sign she felt.

She walked into the apartment quite upbeat but things changed as soon as she got into Hayes' apartment. She took off her shoes by the door.

"This nice, can I have water for drink?" She asked. The response from Hayes was a hard slap from the back of his hand to her cheek.

"Did I ask you to fucking talk? Dirty whore. I am Alf Hayes. Alf fucking Hayes. Take your clothes off."

"Maybe I leave now," a nervous Ploy uttered. This angered Hayes further.

"YOU TALK WHEN ALF HAYES TELL YOU TO."

He pushed her over and slapped her ass as hard as he could.

"You fucking love it!" he shouted. He laughed a grotesque laugh as he ripped her top off and got out his hand cuffs. Before she knew it her left hand was cuffed to a pole that Hayes had especially installed right by the bed. She was naked on the bed and Hayes slapped her again.

"No more noise, no more slaps. *Khaw jai*?" Ploy nodded. Hayes laughed and shouted out "Alf Hayes, hooker trainer. I'm Bangkok's answer to Barbara Woodhouse, the famous dog obedience trainer!" He laughed the words to himself.

Hayes began to undress and he just stood there totally naked looking at Ploy. Ploy could barely see his small hard dick under the rolls of fat from his protruding gut.

"Now love, I'm gonna put something in your mouth. If you don't suck it well I will slap you so hard your kids will be born dizzy." He gave her what he considered a playful slap on the thigh, but still hard enough to leave a temporary red mark.

"Open wide love." Hayes rammed his cock in and Ploy momentarily struggled to get any kind of rhythm. Hayes raised his hand in a threatening gesture and somehow she managed to focus and perform.

"Ooooh fucking lovely. Hello hello, looks like we got another of Alf's favourite tarts!" At this Hayes gave her an almost tender stroke. Ploy felt relieved, Hayes seemed to have calmed down. Just do as Hayes said and she should be ok she thought.

After a few minutes Hayes pulled out.

"Not too fast darling, we don't want your mouth to have all the fun."

With crude gestures and probing fingers Hayes asked if she enjoyed anal sex. Ploy told him no, Hayes laughed.

"When you're with Alf Hayes you're a 3-holer love." Three-holer was Hayes' crude way of describing women who would have anal sex with him as well as blow jobs and the more traditional sex. Hayes laughed and over the next 10-15 minutes he continued to do as he wanted to Ploy, finishing in the '3rd' hole.

"We can't risk you getting pregnant darling."
As he pulled out he squeezed her ass and gave another hard slap.

"Welcome to Alf Hayes! 3-hole Ploy they should start calling you." He threw 3000 baht on the bed and looked at her with utter disgust.

"Clean yourself up and get out you filthy filthy skank. Shut the door when you leave." With that Hayes left her alone in his apartment and returned to the planning of his big drug deal.

Bob had done some initial research and found that not only were there not many private investigators in Bangkok but that when you did find one they tended to be relatively expensive. This he felt would exclude many ordinary people from using their services. He also discovered that many of them were Thai ex-police officers, not only was their spoken English mediocre at best, but Bob considered the sort of folks who wanted to hire a PI in Bangkok might not want to involve anyone connected to the police even in the smallest capacity. Bob and Susie had begun to seriously discuss how they might operate, on a sort of 'no job too small' basis. They would always do initial inquiries either free of charge or at minimal cost. Only if they decided they could take the case would charges begin to be incurred. This was where Bob felt his idea was pure genius. His charges would be means-tested so that people paid according to what they could afford. He hadn't sorted out a fee structure but this was going to be his unique selling point, even the lowest paid people in Bangkok would be able to employ Bob Lowe PI.

Bob and Susie sat outside one of their regular drinking establishments, chatting over their plans. As the hot season had properly arrived, Bangkok's air was beginning to thin, the heat was becoming oppressive. Day by day you could feel the intensity of the sun increasing and Bob knew that his usual battles with the heat and sweat would soon reach critical levels. As Bob sat there he had begun to admit to himself that he found Susie very comfortable to be around. He could talk to her honestly and without the sort of farcical language modifications that had begun to become part of his normal speech with women, the result of years chatting up bar girls with woefully substandard levels of spoken English.

Alf Hayes was in a permanent swagger these days, he felt he was finally on the verge of becoming a proper big shot. He was developing a friendship with a real businessman in Valeriy Dublachenko. All good criminals needed that blur between their criminal life and a genuine and impressive business interest. Dublachenko, he felt, was his door to the business elite in Bangkok. He was also on a high after his encounter with young Ploy. The look of pure terror in her eyes was a big turn on for Hayes, giving him an awesome feeling of power. He was THE Alf Hayes. He mattered. He wanted to shout it from the kerbs and down the *sois*. He saw Bob sat with Susie and as he walked over to them he was approached by a waitress who knew him. Alf gave her ass a squeeze with both hands and then slapped her away with the instructions to get him his usual cold one.

"Bob Lowe! Of all the whores you could be sat

with you're here with the maddest cunt of them all! What you playing at geezer?"

Bob didn't know how to react to this. He gave a feeble chuckle and replied "Alright Alf."

"How's tricks Bob?" Alf virtually ignored Susie, a cursory nod was as far as he would go to acknowledge her existence.

"Oh you know Alf. Same Same. Knees are getting better."

Alf wasn't really interested as he took his first large swig of the beer that had been delivered.

"Lovely piece of ass," he said as the girl walked away from the table. Susie looked at Bob to see his reaction.

"Yeh, terrific," he replied rather feebly.

Susie was not impressed. She had started to see a different side to Bob, but within minutes of Hayes joining them Bob had returned to his Bangkok chauvinistic and misogynistic stereotyped role.

She was clearly annoyed.

"Anyway Bob, I've got to dash. Meeting a friend for an early dinner." It was the first lie Susie had told Bob in the recent days of their new friendship.

Bob uttered a seemingly disinterested "See ya Susie love" as she made her hasty exit. She was still in earshot when Alf asked "What you doing with that mad bitch? Have you lost all self-respect?"

"Come on Alf." Bob's attempt to defend Susie's honour was again rather pathetic and Alf moved the conversation on to show that he really wasn't remotely interested in the likes of Susie Hoare.

He told Bob about his new find, the young Ploy.

"I'll have her trained in no time mate."

He explained that with a combination of the back of

his hand and some of his high quality *ya ice* he'd have her doing whatever he wanted.

"Always keep some good quality pussy nearby. That's why you don't see Alf Hayes trying to tap a bit of Susie Hoare."

"Now come on Alf. She's ok really." Bob was trying to get more forceful in his defence of Susie.

"Fuck me mate, you *are* actually trying to get into Susie's panties! Is that how low you've sunk? Dipping your dick into Susie fucking Hoare? Fucking unreal." There was utter scorn and disgust in Hayes' face as he spat out these words.

Bob went on to explain that he was about to go into a sort of informal business with Susie, a soft launch of 'Lowe Investigations', an affordable PI service available for all.

Hayes couldn't control himself, and begun to laugh hysterically.

"You could not make it up! Bangkok's two biggest *farang* losers starting up in business!"

Lowe began to laugh with him. A desperate attempt to appear he was a self-deprecating fellow with a good sense of humour. He was sure that his old buddy Alf Hayes was just having a bit of good old fashioned British banter.

"Why you fucking laughing?" Hayes suddenly took on a more sinister tone.

"Well you know. Me and Suse, PIs. It's quite funny really I suppose." Lowe replied.

"Funny?! It's more than fucking funny mate. It's end game. You've reached the low point. Get it? Low point!"

He laughed more and Lowe didn't quite know how to respond to this slightly random attack. He felt angry inside but utterly powerless to react. He said nothing. Hayes looked at him, pinched face, with a pitied look like one might give to an injured rat limping through the litter on a Bangkok *soi*.

"Look at you here. Two bandaged knees. What kind of utter loser undergoes two knee ops to make me 100k."

He laughed again.

"What?"

Bob replied, confused but also fighting a desire to break down in tears.

"Yeh you heard me. You think I'd go to all that hassle for 5k? You total moron. I'm Alf Hayes mate. I'm big time. THIS IS MY FUCKING *SOI*, IN MY FUCKING CITY."

Hayes was in a full-on rant and he stood up and scowled at Bob.

"And you'll pay for my fucking beer."

Hayes walked away laughing. Bob sat there, motionless. Shell shocked. A tear ran down his right cheek, mixing with a bead of sweat and dripping down leaving a wet patch on his corduroy trousers.

TWENTY-EIGHT

Ting my sweet wonderful Ting,

I am beside myself with worry now. I have wandered these streets for 3 days hoping for a sight of you, and what a vision of godliness that would be! I have also returned to the airport at the same time each day just in case we had the dates muddled up. What upsets me the most is the idea that you are out there worrying about me and wondering where I am. I hope you know that I am searching for you. I will never stop Ting. Never. I will find you, I will rescue you. We will be together. Scotty and Ting forever.

I know how strong our chemistry is and I can sense you. Sense you are thinking of me. The only thing that keeps me going is thinking of the life we will have together. I am still certain that we will look back on this as an extraordinary story that highlights how much it was meant to be. How I nearly lost my Ting, not once, but twice, but we still conquered those barriers. I am sure our connection is strong enough that I can will you to be where I will be, that I can transmit a message to you. There is a large Big C on the edge of town Ting, everyday I will be there at 9am, and every day I will think hard about this. Big C. 9am. Ting. Scotty. Love. Please Ting hear this message. I can't wait until I see you again and make sweet love to you again. SMIII

Hayes had arranged to meet Andrei for a drink. Andrei had a lot of questions; Hayes needed to put his mind at ease. This was turning out beautifully Big Alf thought. Andrei was clearly a bit nervous, but who wouldn't be getting involved in the world of Alf Hayes. Hayes felt a bit of fear worked in his favour. It would mean Andrei would follow every instruction, strictly to the letter. The last thing Hayes wanted was some kind of maverick who might think for himself. As a test Hayes asked Andrei to meet him at 7pm. Hayes himself arrived at 6.50pm and sat with a view of the door. He was delighted to see Andrei walk in at 6.56pm.

"First test passed. Early, but not too early to stand out." Hayes offered his hand to the younger Russian. Andrei smiled and thanked Alf.

"You're in the big time with Alf Hayes mate. Following my detailed instructions to the letter keeps us both happy," Hayes added with a patronising air.

They ordered two beers and made idle small talk for a few minutes. Hayes tried to impress Andrei with talk of his many female conquests in town. He made it clear that if Andrei played his cards right he could pick up some of Alf's cast offs. "I'll even share up a bit of prime pussy mate, I'm that kind of guy. Alf Hayes looks after his mates."

"Thanks," Andrei flashed a grin he had been

working on, innocent and shy with a hint of fear. 'Alf, I have to admit I am quite nervous about all this."

"Andy, Andy. That's good. A little nervousness is a good thing, trust me. You'll be fine. Alf Hayes doesn't just pick out anybody. I can see you've got what it takes. I can see a bit of a young Alf Hayes in you."

"Wow! Thanks," said Andrei, this time flashing his best proud grin.

"We've got details to thrash out, and I've got lots to do behind the scenes, I won't worry you about that though." Hayes looked from side to side and took on a serious tone. Andrei was battling laughter at times. Alf Hayes acted like someone who had watched too many bad movies.

Hayes explained the beautifully simple process.

"Simplicity is key."

He informed his young charge that a simple plan and a strong eye for detail was what made Alf Hayes so successful. Then Alf delivered the line he had carefully practised.

"Yeh I run this town, but don't believe the rumours mate, I look after my trusted allies, so you got nothing to worry about."

He expected this to be the line that would ensure Andrei would be too terrified to try anything funny.

Andrei listened intently. A young student lapping up every word from his wise old teacher. Alf would have him drive from Bangkok in a mini-van emblazoned with "Elite Myanmar Tours." He would cross the border with few difficulties, Alf would see to that. When over the border a contact would meet him and direct him on the 2-hour drive to the small town that had the central processing plant for the best *ya ice* in South East Asia. They would pack out the van for him, Andrei need not worry about that at all. In fact he could relax with a bowl of noodle soup. Officially Andrei was picking up hiking supplies and would simply drive himself back to Thailand. When safely over the border he would be met by Hayes at an agreed location. Hayes would have luxury transport for Andrei to travel back to Bangkok, and the mini-van would be taken by Hayes direct to his storage locations.

"The less time you spend with the merchandise, the better mate. We minimise your risk. Let Alf Hayes take those risks."

Andrei did his relieved face. Hayes explained that Andrei's risk was actually non-existent since Hayes had contacts at the border. Hayes gave Andrei the full address details of his production centre in deepest Myanmar and contact details for Rung who would meet Andrei just over the border and would take control of everything. Hayes felt this would really help to put the youngster at ease.

"Fuck this is well organised!" Andrei sounded suitably impressed.

"Too right mate. You're with Alf Hayes now mate. Professional. Prepare to get rich, and then you can get very high." Hayes laughed and summoned over a waitress. He placed his hand on her ass and pinched.

"Two more sweetheart." Hayes sat back with a typically smug grin on his face. Everything really was falling into place. He could feel his stock rising. He looked at the Russian,

"Stick with Alf Hayes and you'll be fine."

Although Valeriy rarely got involved with the specific day to day dealings that Andrei 1 was involved with, he did ask for a report back over the Hayes situation. Valeriy preferred to keep detached from the ins and outs unless it was critically important. Like many great business leaders, Valeriy would only interfere in the event of an emergency or a big strategic decision. Largely he trusted the Andreis and Nat to get on with the details and he found this a good way to earn their loyalty. The trust and respect was mutual.

The last time Valeriy had got involved with the grubbier side of the business was 3 years previously over the troubling case of Alexis Mikahailov, a rare bad appointment that Andrei1 and Nat had made. There had been a growing Russian presence in and around Bangkok with good drug marketing potential. Russian backpackers, and other middle and even some higher earners spending extended periods of time in Thailand. Nat had noticed this (through his small focus group and market research) to the extent that he had included a young Russian as part of his group, such was his belief in the potential to exploit this market. Nat, supported by Andrei, theorised that Russians with their strong sense of national pride and of course the language problems many of them had in Thailand, would feel more comfortable with a Russian dealer. Nat felt they could take most of the Russian business by adding a Russian to their team of dealers, and they would then be well-placed to cash in as the Russian market grew.

After some extensive research Andrei found Alexis Mikhailov, and he seemed to fit the bill perfectly. He was thirty years old from a relatively wealthy family (the nature of their wealth was unclear). He took the work seriously and showed genuine care and attention to detail in everything he did. After 6 months he had indeed began to attract a vast amount of the Russian business through two street outreach dealers. Profits were showing a considerable rise and it was almost all down to the efforts of Alexis. The success however, began to go to Alexis' head and after a couple of short holidays in the South of Thailand, he began to talk about taking control of the Phuket scene and tapping into the local Thai markets.

"With my success, why limit myself to Russians? Why limit myself to Bangkok and Pattaya?" He repeatedly said to Andrei.

Andrei fed this straight back to Valeriy Dublachenko who instructed him to keep a very close eye on Alexis, to keep him informed, and to be ready to act fast if needed. It was only a week later that Alexis contacted Andrei to say that he was hiding out in Phuket as he had got into some difficulties. Andrei ordered Alexis to remain in Phuket, and Andrei himself got himself on a flight to Phuket as soon as he could.

The trouble was two-fold. Not only had Alexis been openly trying to sell drugs, alerting the local drug dealers, but he'd also made inappropriate and vulgar comments to the wife of the local drug dealing chief. Valeriy had instructed Andrei to take swift and final action. He knew from experience that if you don't take care of these things instantly they can run out of control. Andrei hugged Alexis on reaching his condo and with a swift move of his right hand administered a lethal dose of heroin mixed with cocaine. Another sad episode of a young backpacker getting caught up in the Thailand drug scene and overdoing it. Valeriy had authorised Andrei to make a significant peace gesture to *Khun* Suparat who ran the Phuket scene. A culturally sensitive face to face apology from Andrei, while quietly leaving a few hundred thousand baht on the table. It was a simple gesture that required few words or explanation and it quickly smoothed things over.

Andrei and Suparat enjoyed a drink together and Andrei invited him to dinner with his boss Valeriy on his next visit to Bangkok. The slick way this whole issue was dealt with showed the business acumen of Valeriy Dublachenko and his associates, as well as his innate ability to assess a situation.

In terms of the Alf Hayes situation, Andrei was merely using Valeriy as a sounding board to talk through their plans, which were even more simple than Hayes', but contrastingly, they had been thought through to the last detail. Andrei figured that it would be pretty simple to persuade someone to stop working with the vile Alf Hayes in favour of real professionals. Hayes certainly had the potential to be something of a loose cannon and Val would likely approve of the decision to have him 'removed', but he preferred not to resort to that solution. He found the Brit to be quite amusing, light relief on the occasions that he bumped into him and whilst that wasn't reason to keep him around, it was certainly a reason to try and avoid a mortal solution.

They agreed to assess how Hayes reacted to having his business wrestled from him and then come to a decision.

The plan worked beautifully, as expected. Once Andrei was over the border with Rong he simply negotiated a vastly improved deal. He had a large cash payment upfront as a gift from Valeriy Dublachenko as well as gifts for Rong's wife and family – a nice touch that Rong felt was classy. He explained as much as he needed in terms of business and credibility and detailed how he could ensure that Alf Hayes would not be an issue. Unknown to Hayes, Val had used some contacts within Myanmar to guarantee that the small time petty criminal Alf Hayes would not be allowed into the country, in the unlikely event that he attempted to go and confront Rong.

Rong jumped at the deal and two days later when Hayes waited at the allotted rendezvous, Andrei simply didn't show up. Hayes shinned it back to Bangkok, he initially assumed that Andrei and his haul had been arrested at the border and he wanted to be well out of the area. He waited patiently, checking the papers for news of a drug bust, but heard nothing. He also got no reply from his repeated texts to both Andrei and Rong. After 3 days Hayes began to wonder if there really was any possible way that he had been scammed by the pair.

TWENTY-NINE

On Scotty's next visit to see Sargent Niki at the main Khon Kaen police station, Niki decided it was time to act. Scotty was increasingly becoming known as an annoying nuisance around town. Niki had heard about *farang* like this before, but ordinarily the penny would drop, they would realise what was going on and leave sheepishly and embarrassed. After all, who would want to admit they had fallen for such a blatant and obvious con? Niki thought that he would like to meet this pair. It was pretty impressive to have effectively stolen such a large sum of money and yet still have the victim insist that there was no theft!

Scotty walked into the police station, sweating profusely, a mini rucksack on his back and clutching a pile of the 'MISSING' fliers with the picture of *Khun* Gift and the absurd request for information if someone had seen a woman who resembled her. As soon as the receptionist saw Marshall in the doorway he immediately called for Niki and signalled for Marshall to take a seat.

Khun Niki strutted towards Scotty and with a confident air said

"Come this way please Mr Marshall."

Scotty felt a shiver run down his spine. Usually Niki would just tell him in reception that there was no news. He was sure there must be some development. He felt terrified, yet also excited. Had Ting been found?

"Certainly. Is there news? Has the investigation found Ting?" Scotty asked anxiously.

"Let's sit down and talk."

"Ting!" Marshall let out a quiet moan.

Khun Niki led Marshall into one of the few quiet meeting rooms they had. It wasn't actually an interrogation room but it had that feel. A grey stone floor and dirty walls of a vague beige colour. The light was a fluorescent bulb that was losing its power and the air conditioning spluttered creating a coolish yet uncomfortably humid atmosphere. The sweat continued to drip down Marshall's face.

"Would you like some water?" Niki asked politely.

"Water! Just tell me where my darling Ting is!"

"Well, I'm afraid..." Niki began to speak.

"NO! NO! Please no! Ting! My Ting!"

"Mr Marshall, please. There is no news on Ting. You must accept this is not a police matter, yet."

"Yet? What do you mean by that?" Marshall quizzed the policeman.

"Mr Marshall, I have received significant complaints that you are harassing people in town."

Marshall looked genuinely confused.

"Harassing?"

"Yes, and these posters you have made. They are almost certainly illegal. You can't just use an actress for your own advert in this way." Niki was trying hard to be very stern.

"Advert?" Marshall continued to feel lost in this conversation.

"You have given me no choice but to officially warn you. The next time I have to speak to you it will be to arrest you for disturbing the peace and wasting police time."

"But, Ting..." Marshall seemed to lose his energy as his spoke.

"My advice to you would be to return to Bangkok and begin your enquiries in the bar you met Ting. Someone must know where she has run off to with your cash."

Niki had already stood and opened the door, motioning for Marshall to leave. "You should consider trying to officially report this crime to the Bangkok police."

As Marshall walked back to his hotel he thought long and hard about what the policeman had said. He began to realise that Niki's words made some sense. What was he doing continuing the desperate and forlorn search of this strange city. Return to Bangkok, yes Niki was right. Ting would surely also think to return to the very place that they had first met. Surely he would be able to locate Pinky there too. Marshall already began to feel much more upbeat. He realised that remaining in Khon Kaen was a crazy decision he had made, letting his emotional state take over from his logical brain. He would write a letter to Sargent Nik and thank him for helping him see things clearly again, and ultimately helping him to be reunited with his dear Ting. Niki would be at the wedding, Marshall would insist on it. The Khon Kaen cop was just another bizarre sub plot in the remarkable Ting and Scotty love story. Step aside Romeo and Juliet, Ting and Scotty are the natural successors.

Hayes was a mess. A lethal cocktail of emotions roared through his system – anger, bewilderment, humiliation and pure depression. He swung from furious murderous rage to moping around feeling sorry for himself. He'd lost not just all his spare cash with that upfront investment, but also his dignity and his feeling of manhood. Of course, no one in his circle of friends knew anything, but in Hayes' mind people were watching him and laughing at him. He'd stopped obsessively trying to call Andrei or Rong. That line of attack was clearly futile and he'd been fobbing off his customers with 'logistical issues'. It wasn't long before the customers just stopped calling him, not because they had moved on from smoking or injecting *ya ice*, but because they had obviously found another supplier. This further enraged him, as he assumed that Andrei had managed to get his stolen supply onto the streets of Bangkok. Alf Hayes' streets. When Hayes managed to calm down and have some clarity of thought, he realised his Russian friend Valeriy Dublachenko was his best, perhaps only chance of getting in touch with the younger Russian who had so foolishly scammed him.

In the first few days he had been unsuccessful in finding Valeriy, he had no contact number or address. He had always just tended to bump into him occasionally in the same quiet bar above the convenience store. He was now in the habit of going there every night for at least one or two hours in the hope of running into him. It was a full week after he had returned to Bangkok that he finally ran into Valeriy. Alf was starting to feel a little calmer, though there were still bouts of rage. He strolled down the *soi* for his usual drink and search for Dublachenko.

There had been some unseasonal rain which had left the road damp with a few puddles. Rather than cool from the rain, the air seemed to have a muggy humidity that didn't sit well with Alf's overweight frame. He tried his best to dodge the puddles but stepped on a loose paving stone causing some significant splash-back up his right thigh. With almost musical timing he then got dripped on from above, both events serving to push him further away from the calmer end of the Alf Hayes emotion meter. The only saving grace for Hayes was that it had just been raining so he could feel confident that the water that had so rudely attacked him was more akin to rainwater than sewage. He walked into the bar and his emotions went into overdrive when he saw Valeriy sat at the bar with a large whisky in his hand.

"OI! Val Double!" Hayes roared.
There was no reaction from Valeriy although as Hayes got closer he shouted again. "Oi! Val!"

"Oh hello Mr Hayes. How are you?" Valeriy spoke with his usual offhand indifference.

"I'm fucking furious mate. I need to find that cunt Andrei you set me up with."

"What? Who?"

"And-er-fucking-rei. That's who. Your mate. He's got himself in way too deep mate. I'm Alf Hayes."

"Oh the young Russian guy. I can't say he's a friend of mine. You need to calm down I think." Valeriy was toying with him now.

"CALM DOWN! Do you know who you are fucking talking to?"

Valeriy smirked, which initially did little to help the situation. He signalled to the barman to get Hayes a drink. An imposing bouncer approached Hayes and eventually got him to quiet down. He apologised to Valeriy.

"I'm sorry Val mate. I know it's not your fault. You're just a property developer, but I fear for this Andrei. He's scammed the wrong guy I'm afraid."
Hayes then tried to give some pathetic analogy of Val being conned in the property business and then strongly hinted that messing with a big-shot drug lord like Hayes would unfortunately be terminal.
Valeriy of course looked shocked.

"Oh dear. Let me contact some Russian friends and try to get in contact with him. Shouldn't be a problem." Said Valeriy.

"Cheers Val mate. Listen I'm sorry to get you involved with this. Don't worry you won't have any more bother with this, but if you can just get me his contact details."

They had an amicable chat, but Valeriy was finding Hayes rather tiresome on this occasion. He explained to Hayes that he had some business calls to Europe to make, but took Hayes' number and promised to pass it on and get hold of Andrei for him.

This scenario was nothing of a surprise. In fact when Valeriy had discussed how things might play out in his recent management meeting with Andrei and Nat, this sort of rage fuelled delusion was the most likely. They had simulated a number of options, and as usual Valeriy stated he would prefer no bloodshed, but of course he had 100% faith in the pair's ability to manage the situation. Naturally he would approve of Hayes being permanently removed from the equation but only if other avenues had been exhausted.

Hayes remained in the bar for another couple of drinks. Confidence returned, he shook his head to himself and muttered on numerous occasions "I'm Alf Hayes. I'm Alf fucking Hayes."

Valeriy left and immediately called Nat to arrange an emergency 'board' meeting with both Andreis. Andrei 2 would no doubt be highly critical of their hesitancy and indecisiveness with Alf Hayes. Valeriy himself had become slightly concerned by Hayes' anger and feared that the Londoner might just be too stupid to realise the danger he was getting himself into. Nat chaired the meeting with his Russian colleagues. All mobiles were switched off and placed into a box. Valeriy always wanted to do anything he could to limit the possibility of anyone being aware that these meetings took place. Nat spoke first

"Agenda item 1, Alf Hayes."

THIRTY

Marshall was back in Bangkok and although he still refused to believe that Ting and Pinky had scammed him he was finding it increasingly difficult to motivate himself to search for Ting. On those days when he didn't search or plan, he was overcome with guilt. Was he admitting to himself that all hope for him and Ting was lost?

My Dear Ting,

I have raced back to Bangkok. I realised my search in Khon Kaen was becoming futile and frankly the local police were worse than useless. Then I realised, my sweet Ting would have headed back to Bangkok if you felt you couldn't locate me in Khon Kaen. I didn't know where to start, I did go back to that bar where we first met, but of course they knew nothing. They seemed to be only familiar with these so-called 'bar girls'. A sweet flower like Ting probably isn't even aware what that term means. Working girls Ting. Hookers. So I could hardly be surprised to find that they didn't know where you were. I dare say you only went there a few times for a social drink. Oh my sweet naïve Ting, strolling into a bar like that in that part of town just to have a quiet drink. I will find you, we will be together. I hope that wherever you are that you still hope to be with me. Your true love. I know that I am that to you. I know. You know. Of course I worry Ting, time is racing along with no news. So I know it must be the influence of your brother. I hope he is not trying to turn your mind against me. Be strong Ting. Do not let them influence you. What if they have lied to you? Told you that I didn't turn up in Khon Kaen? That I changed my mind. I am terrified that you might believe them. But no, I am sure Pinky would have not allowed that to happen. A true friend like Pinky would never let you believe any lies. I know Pinky will be doing what she can to get you back for me. To me. To us. We will be together Ting. It's written in the stars.

Your loving fiancé,

SM III

Hayes was delirious when Valeriy rang him to say he had got in touch with Andrei. Delirious but still full of rage. Ideas flashed through Hayes' mind about how he might deal with Andrei. The fact that Val was calling him, perhaps there was a reasonable explanation. Everything could still be sorted. Hayes could be a forgiving man. He didn't need to go all Alf Hayes on Andrei. But lessons had to be learnt.
He waited for the Russian to respond.

"Yes Alf. I don't want to get involved of course, but he is Russian and you met him through me. I feel a sense of duty, you understand?"

"Of course Val mate, again I'm sorry. So what did Andy say?" an anxious Hayes asked.

"He said he can explain everything and that he hopes you can both sort it out. Give him a chance Alf. Maybe he is scared?" Valeriy felt deliciously naughty, playing with the pathetic Brit like this.

"He'd better be scared. He's got in too deep mate. But Alf Hayes is a fair man. I'd rather sort it all amicably. I run these streets mate." Hayes' swagger was starting to return.

"I'm sure Andrei will be relieved to hear." Valeriy would have laughed if he were the laughing type. He wasn't. Valeriy Dublachenko doesn't joke.

Valeriy explained to Alf where and when he should meet Andrei. A small bar on *Soi* 8 that Alf hadn't been to, but was a popular haunt with some of the city's Russian expats. This was the approach that Val had recommended, which Andrei wasn't totally comfortable with. Andrei felt that someone as irrelevant as Hayes could simply be forgotten about. Valeriy Dublachenko always impressed upon his charges to leave no loose ends. He hadn't got where he was today by leaving issues unresolved. Even small ones. Sure Hayes was pretty unimportant in the grand scheme of things, but he was an irritant and sometimes even the smallest irritant could do some serious damage.

"Consider the mosquito," was a regular catchphrase of Valeriy's when speaking with Andrei. He had always had a fascination with mosquitoes. This tiny insect caused absolute devastation, a million deaths a year. And more strikingly he had read that the mosquito just bit people because it could. "The mosquito has no need to bite." He would continue his story. His point didn't need explaining but he did anyway. He pointed out to Andrei and Nat that even Alf Hayes has the potential to be a mosquito. "In this business you may laugh at people. You may pity them. You may consider them an irrelevance, but you may not underestimate them." A simple piece of advice that had worked very nicely for him.

Valeriy Dublachenko hadn't underestimated anyone since he was a 15-year-old at high school in South Moscow. He was already something of a tough guy and had the reputation of being someone to be feared. At the time he had the arrogance of youth, he was good looking and attracted the attention of girls through the school. There was one he was particularly keen on, the delightful Evgeniya Popov, a Russian of Bulgarian heritage. To Valeriy she was perfect. Intelligent, strong-willed, attractive with the most beautiful smile, and flowing auburn hair. She was also dating someone, in the way 15-year-olds dated, the slightly nerdy Alex Vasiliev. It amused Valeriy why she would even look twice at the pasty-faced Alex with his oh so pale skin and ghostly blonde, almost white hair. It just made Evgeniya even more interesting to him. Valeriy asked her out again and again. Eventually with a mixture of frustration at being asked out so often, and perhaps being slightly impressed with his persistence, Evgeniya accepted. Valeriy was ecstatic, he was surprised it took her so long to accept, but again it just made her more interesting. She was so aloof at first, even to Valeriy Dublachenko, that took guts. They had arranged to hang out after school in a local café. When friends asked Valeriy if Alex knew, he laughed.

"That nerd!? I couldn't care less what he knows."

Two days later, the day before the date with Evgeniya, Valeriy was ambushed on his way home from school by three people, assumed to be three of Alex's friends. One of them was a 17-year-old youth boxing champion who was hoping to make it onto a future Russian Olympic team. They battered Val and left him limping home with a broken nose and blood dripping down his face, not to mention feeling humiliated. He couldn't go to see Evgeniya like this. The story that was spread around school was that Valeriy had gone to Alex and told him to back off and that Evgeniya was now his. Evgeniya was furious and never spoke to Valeriy again. He felt utterly hopeless. Yet he never forgot that feeling, it shaped the person he had become. He would never underestimate anyone again, ever.

In the days that followed his run-in with Alf, Bob felt seriously melancholic. He moped around with a deep feeling of lethargy resulting from obvious depression. He started to ponder that for years he had been denying to himself just how grim his life had become. There was no denying it now. One of his 'best mates' was a low-life who had used him in the most callous of ways and clearly had zero respect for him. Everything now came to the forefront of his mind. He had not been in a relationship for 15 years. It had also been 15 years since he'd had sex that he hadn't paid for. He'd heard himself for years explain why he preferred this system. Convincing himself that he had chosen this path, as a preference as he 'wasn't really the relationship type'. He had been discussing this with people (people who he met hanging around Nana and *Soi* Cowboy and therefore who invariably ended up agreeing with him).

"It's just another form of service really. No different from getting a foot scrub, or someone to do your laundry."

On the occasions when he spoke in this candid way with people who didn't approve, Bob took the stance that these people just didn't understand Thai culture. There was even one occasion when Bob explained that since most of these girls were from a poor background in Thailand's North East, and tended to send money home to support their families, that he was in fact doing his bit to fight poverty in Thailand.

"There is so much inequality in Thailand, it's important we help to redistribute wealth from Bangkok to *Isaan*." A classic Bob Lowe stock phrase that he had used many times. He had even started to believe it, but now deep down he started to realise just how sad his life had become.

He rarely admitted to others, even close friends, the game he played in his mind. He would pretend he was chatting up a girl, and having to charm her. When he woke up in the morning he would imagine he was in bed with his wife and they were deeply in love. In the 12 or so hours he spent with these girls he would try to have conversations as if they were a couple in a long-term relationship. He would enquire about her family and he would daydream about planning a visit for a weekend. He'd even suggest it sometimes, though he knew it was never going to happen.

The sad truth was that Bob had now become such a pathetic individual that he didn't even find it that easy to pick up a hooker. He usually had to wait until late into the night when the women were getting more desperate and so he tended to find himself shopping in the low-end of the market. But even the low-end cheapest hookers almost never wanted a repeat performance with Bob Lowe. Financially he was never going to be a provider. He smelt bad and his apartment was pretty miserable with limited facilities. If he'd even had a pool then some girls may have gone back for more, just to spend a few hours in the morning relaxing by a nice pool. Bob was never likely to spend money on living in that sort of condo though.

He told himself this would be a fresh start. He'd stop drinking, get fit, stop picking up hookers. However, in this most depressed of states he knew only one way to get by – bury himself in alcohol. He rolled over in bed and saw perhaps the lowest end hooker he had ever picked up. She showed clear signs of early pregnancy and her back was covered in scabs and scars. He could see that her face was pock marked now the makeup was gone and she had crooked teeth, with one tooth missing completely. The marks on her arm suggested she was an injecting drug user and on her right leg were signs of burns and a mediocre skin graft to repair the damage. He felt ashamed and disgusted with himself. He couldn't even remember her name and when she woke up her hangover gave her an aggressive nature. She slapped and punched Bob, an argument erupted and she demanded 2000 baht. Bob tried to negotiate this, which was a big mistake. She hurled her shoe at him and in the end he paid her 3000 baht. The additional 1000 baht was to cover the cost of the high heels that had suffered damage. He was relieved when he closed the door behind her.

He sat back on his bed and took a deep sigh. He wasn't actually suicidal, but he did wonder whether he should be. He texted Susie. 'Hit a new low last night, so depressed.' He waited for a reply. He needed to talk. He checked the time: 8:51am, Susie should be awake by now. After ten minutes he texted again in a desperate attempt to elicit a reply. 'Hope it's not too early.' This did the trick.

'No worries Bob, hope you're ok.' She followed this with a sad face and a teary faced emoticon. In recent weeks Bob had started to confide in Susie all his horrible truths. He felt like she didn't judge him and the truth was her life was at an equally low point. They often got into a competition to see whose life was worse. Bob felt this was one of those rare situations when he won something in life. Even Susie's pathetic life hadn't yet plumbed the depths of Bob Lowe's. Susie suggested they meet for lunch, and this did help to calm Bob and give him a semblance of purpose, at least for a few hours.

THIRTY-ONE

The meeting between Hayes and Andrei was set for 8pm on a Wednesday evening. Hayes arrived early and approached with caution. He also knew he had to contain his anger, even though he felt this young Russian had acted in an extremely naïve and stupid way.

Alf sat in the bar and looked around. He wanted to try and avoid a scene and he didn't like being in unfamiliar territory, but if he had to teach Andrei a lesson then so be it. When Andrei walked in Alf had managed to calm himself to the extent that he didn't attack the Russian as soon as he could. They exchanged pleasantries which seemed quite bizarre given the circumstances.

"Right sunshine. Enough of this. You're lucky I don't just tear your fucking throat out. You've got some serious explaining to do. Now." Hayes was feeling confident and he felt this obvious confidence would help to intimidate Andrei.

"Mr Hayes, this is not an ideal situation, but I hope we can sort it all out amicably." Andrei spoke with a calm assuredness and a level of English that momentarily caught Hayes off guard.

"You what?!" replied Hayes.

"I would like to financially clear things up and reimburse you."

"You'll give me a million dollars' worth of high grade Burmese *ya ice* is what you will do." Hayes tried his best to remain calm but his voice was rising.

Andrei let out an audible chuckle.

"I'm afraid that isn't possible but we would like to see that you are compensated." Hayes was confused by the cool and calm Russian. This was not what he expected.

"Are you taking the piss mate? Have you any idea who I am?"

"Mr Hayes, the people I represent are prepared to return your capital outlay and have agreed to a most generous additional $10,000 to compensate you for your inconvenience."

With that, Hayes slammed his hand hard on the table.

"I'M ALF FUCKING HAYES!"

Two muscular security personnel immediately flanked the table. Andrei continued to speak in this calm manner.

"I'm going to have to ask you to be quiet. Are you prepared to accept this offer?"

Hayes was apoplectic with rage.

"No I am fucking not. I'm ALF HAYES. H-A-Y-E-S, HAYES! And you are a fucking dead man."

The smaller of the two security guards moved and placed his hand around Alf's throat, instantly incapacitating him.

"You be quiet now, ok?"

The small man seemed impossibly strong. Hayes didn't reply as he was struggling for breath. The man repeated in a soft voice.

"You quiet, ok?"

Hayes nodded meekly as he gasped for breath.

"Young Benz's grip is so powerful that he could kill you by suffocation in little more than a minute. Do not make any more noise."

Hayes looked lost and bewildered as Andrei continued to speak. Andrei had had high hopes that he would be able to get Hayes to agree to his suggestion.

"As a show of gratitude to our kind and generous offer, you Mr Hayes will not attempt to sell any more products that might conflict with our business interests. I am sure you will agree this is fair."

Andrei looked at Hayes and waited. Hayes was still trying to get his full lung capacity back. Eventually he raged again.

"FUCK YOU! I. AM. ALF. HAYES!"

With that the larger of the two men delivered a swift blow to the back of Hayes' neck that instantly rendered him unconscious. A disappointed Andrei shook his head.

"You stupid, stupid, man."

Within minutes the two men had taken Hayes out a back door and Andrei approached the barman.

"Sorry about all that."

He slid him a pile of notes and walked out the bar with the same air of confidence that he'd had when he walked in.

Alf Hayes woke to find himself tied to a chair in the middle of a dimly lit basement. His brain was processing at a million miles an hour, so fast and still so angry. So fucking angry that he couldn't channel in on any sensible thought. He needed to focus on a way he could extract himself from this predicament (Hayes wasn't to know that there was no escaping from the clutches of Andrei's goons). He was furious, furious and utterly humiliated. Too angry to notice the floor had been excavated down about two feet deeper than it should have been and that his chair was pushing into the rough foundations of a Bangkok shop house. He was still confused, he didn't really know what was going on. He couldn't work out with any clarity that he had got himself involved with real high-level drug dealers who would waste little time in disposing of the likes of Alf Hayes. Andrei 1 had long gone, he considered himself something of a pacifist and was rarely prepared to actually kill someone. Luckily, Nat and Andrei 2 had a specialist for just that sort of job. *Khun* Suthit (Bom to his friends) had spent his youth in and out of trouble with the police and in and out of prison. His low-level intelligence would have allowed him to be given special attention in many places but in Thailand he just got lost in the system, or lost outside any system. He never graduated high school. His IQ of around 65 made him easily influenced. As a child he committed no end of petty crimes, usually persuaded by other neighbourhood kids. Usually these were thefts from local stores, but as he entered his teenage years he graduated to some violent episodes. The violence gave him a huge thrill and he sought out situations where he could fight. He was 22 when he met Nat who instantly saw Bom as the perfect soldier; strong and malleable. He had slowly worked on Bom's sadistic nature and for the last 5 years he had proved totally reliable. Nat provided him with an apartment and a solid wage. He also saw to it that money was sent monthly to his family in Phitsanulok. Bom's parents were relieved that their son had found work in Bangkok and that it was good enough to help provide for them in their approaching old age. They were also touched that Nat was taking Bom under his wing and helping with daily tasks like financial management that they knew Bom would not be capable of.

Bom treated this job like any other he had done for Nat and Andrei over the years. He walked into the basement room clutching an iced-latte that he had picked up from 7-11 on his way and also carried a small bag of his favourite fried chicken wings. He sat quietly eating his breakfast as Hayes began to summon enough energy to shout.

"Right sunshine, get me the fuck out of here. NOW!"

Bom continued to munch delicately and dextrously at the tiny chicken wings, dwarfed by his large powerful hands.

"You fucking listening?"

"SA-WAT-FUCKING-DI."

Hayes began to wonder if this scruffy looking chap was deaf such was his focus on his coffee and chicken wings.

Bom had always found that when you had a noisy one it was much easier just to quieten them first. Unless he wanted to savour their screams and panic.

Sometimes he got a thrill from that, but today he just wanted to get the job finished. It was annoying trying to kill someone who was shouting and struggling to escape. It also increased the risk of something going wrong or getting himself injured and causing an unnecessary mess. He took a needle from his backpack and walked behind Hayes, jabbing the sharp metal into his neck. The effect took hold almost instantly, Hayes was silenced in a matter of seconds. Bom then removed his equipment from his bag, a large machete style knife, a hammer and other small tools. He was very thorough and although it was highly improbable that Hayes' body would ever be discovered, he liked to do what he could to make identification almost impossible. The first step was to remove the hands. Bom found this a good place to start as in this sitting position the blood would quickly drain down into the rubble onto the floor, making the next tasks more straightforward. With sharp blows of the machete he had both hands clean off. They would be incinerated later that day. This was always the dangerous phase, having to transport body parts around town, so he preferred to take as little as possible. He took an axe to Alf's head and using the hammer smashed out his teeth and cracked his jaw. He then set about dismembering Hayes' corpse into smaller pieces. The smell was unpleasant and Hayes had defecated as his muscles gave way. Bom used copious amounts of bleach that he poured around to dilute the blood and guts and to help with the smell. He always wore a high quality mask, the sort someone might use in an industrial setting, to ensure he didn't pass out from the fumes and stench. With the hands, teeth, and fragments of jaw tightly sealed in a strong plastic rubble bag he began the harder work of tipping bag after bag of rubble onto the basement to prepare it for concrete. It would take him about 4 hours to complete the job and he knew he couldn't afford any mistakes. He covered the rubble with bags of sand and had already completely covered the body. He smoothed the sand over before applying a layer of plastic which would help to seal from the moisture and speed up the curing rate of the concrete. The room had been excavated quite deeply and so when finished, Alf Hayes would be safely under 2-3 feet of flooring, concrete, sand and rubble. By 2pm Bom had smoothed over the whole area, tidied up his equipment and left, taking the hands and jaw of Alf Hayes to be incinerated. Only then would he allow himself some lunch. The incinerated remains would go into another building project, somewhere across the city the following day.

Once the remains had been incinerated and mixed in with a bag of sand ready to be set in concrete within 24 hours, he sent a simple text to Andrei 2 to say he was going to have some food. Andrei understood what this meant. Again, Bom had worked with great efficiency and professionalism. A matter of days later Andrei was standing in the basement, freshly painted with a brand new concrete floor waiting to have the interior design completed. The floor would be covered in wood laminate, with some nice rugs, a gorgeous leather sofa and an imposing desk. Whether the office would ever be fully utilised was essentially irrelevant. Alf Hayes was gone and soon to be forgotten.

THIRTY-TWO

One Year Later

Nong Khai

Khun Jeab woke at 5am, as usual, and touched the photo of her son Note that sat on her bedside table with his necklace draped around it. If only Note could see her now. He would be so happy and so proud of how well her life was panning out. Of course, she believed Note *was* with her. Somewhere. Somehow. She was certain that she would meet him again. She just hoped she would be aware of it when it finally happened. Sometimes she saw a rather cute bird perch itself on the side of the hotel restaurant and wondered. A grey and black bird with a distinctive little tuft of dark hair on the top of its head. It was cheeky too, trying to edge its way toward the bread during the morning breakfast buffet. Jeab would always delicately shoo it away, just in case.

The Riverview Boutique Resort was already proving a wonderful success. Word of mouth was proving a strong tool and guests loved the friendly hospitality as well as the idyllic setting. Jeab liked to wake early so she could be there for the breakfast shift, to chat with guests and help them to organise their days. Ting and Pinky were working harder than they ever remembered, but it was fulfilling work and they were enjoying every minute of it. The resort was giving plenty of opportunities to young people in their province to work there and gain experience in many aspects of the hospitality business. It was Ting and Pinky's own little way of making a difference. The restaurant and bar was gaining a reputation for all the right reasons. Wonderful old-style Thai food and a chilled out vibe, with Friday jazz nights becoming especially popular. After a long day, as the waiting and kitchen staff cleaned up the bar and restaurant, Ting, Pinky, and Jeab would typically sit around a table gazing out at the river with a drink contemplating how good their lives were becoming. They never mentioned the fat American Guy, it was the big unspoken. The elephant in the room. Sure they felt an element of guilt, how could they not? They also felt that his sort deserved to be punished not just for their remarkable stupidity but for their casually exploitative attitude.

Portland, Oregon

Lou-May wheeled her shopping trolley down the corridor of the hostel she had lived in for the last 10 years. She saw her friend Wayne leaving his room.

"Wayne honey, have you had your Pomelo

today?" Wayne laughed. He had the same conversation with Lou-May most days and he had tired of telling her he didn't like Pomelo. In the early days of living in Central Portland Hostel he had many furious arguments with Lou-May about it. She took the topic of Pomelos very seriously. As seriously as Wayne took his obsession with finding a flame-haired Scottish or Irish woman to complete his life. At 45 and living in the Pacific Northwest coast of the USA his chances were thinning by the day.

"How's Scotty today?"

"I dunno Lou-May, not seen him."

Scotty was Wayne's neighbour and had moved into this hostel 8 months earlier. Central Portland Hostel had become something of a home for Portland's misfits; many were ex-army, many were ex-homeless, and some had moderate mental health issues. Rent was as cheap as could be found and the staff who ran it turned a blind eye to much of what went on.

In Room 421 on the 4th floor, Scott Marshall sat on his bed. He had a day-off from his job packing bags and generally helping out at the local Walmart store. The rent was cheap, which was essential. He was saving money to visit 'Madame Hilda', a clairvoyant in Los Angeles who he had read about in a trashy magazine some months earlier. The walls of his room were adorned with pictures of Gift Suriyanka, an actress relatively unknown outside her native Thailand. There was a large wedding photo. Over the face of the bride and groom had crudely been cut a picture of Scotty and Gift. Scotty looked at the picture.

"Keep waiting for me my sweet Ting, I will be with you soon enough."

Available now from Amazon or ZachJBrodsky.com:

'The Mysterious Case of the Missing Tuk-Tuk'
the first in the Bob Lowe Investigation Series.

Stolen tuk tuks. Cheating boyfriends. Scandal in the Ladies' Bridge Club. A lost disco-dancing superstar. If you've got a problem and you don't know which way to turn, then Bob Lowe is your man; Bangkok's newest expat private investigator.

Ex-womaniser and sometime drunk, Bob is desperately trying to clean up his act. His bumbling methods may not be conventional but with his trusted friend and translator, Pat, by his side he may just have finally found his calling in life.

If you enjoy mysteries with a touch of humour and the bizarre then check out the first book in the Bob Lowe PI series.

ZACH J BRODSKY

Zach J Brodsky spent much of his youth traipsing around the world where he was fascinated by observing people and creating absurd back stories in his mind about their lives. The result was the creation of an endless list of characters. He roamed around East and Southern Africa in the early 1990s sneaking into what was Zaire to spend some time with mountain gorillas, and later travelled extensively in South East Asia and the West Coast of the USA. Zach experimented with traditional employment for many years before deciding to base himself in Bangkok where he began to observe all the oddities that Bangkok has to offer, ultimately motivating him to try and patch some characters together in creating his first full novel "Bangkok Delusions".

Zach continues to roam the globe in his own nomadic way, often more in mind than body, but always looking for inspiration for new storylines.

For more information on Zach's books visit www.zachjbrodsky.com and sign up for advance notification on new releases and special offers.

Printed in Great Britain
by Amazon